OUR PATCH

Also by John Hutchins:
The Carved Angel

Our Patch

John Hutchins

With illustrations by
Carol Rea

UNITED WRITERS
Cornwall

UNITED WRITERS PUBLICATIONS LTD
Ailsa, Castle Gate, Penzance, Cornwall.
www.unitedwriters.co.uk

British Library Cataloguing in Publication Data:
A catalogue record for this book is
available from the British Library.

ISBN 9781852001957

Printed and bound in Great Britain by
United Writers Publications Ltd.,
Cornwall.

To my ‘beloved Ma’
– my mother Doris May Hutchins,
née Ruby (1930-2020),
for all her love, support,
laughter and friendship.

Also to my great friend and loyal
doggy companion, Ben, a wonderful
Collie cross, who shared with me
in many adventures.

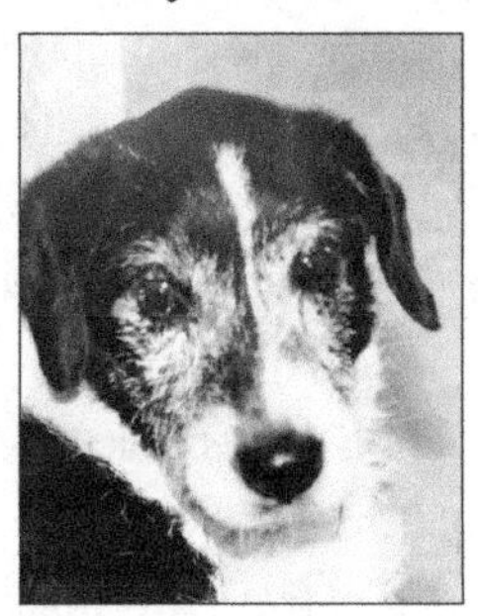

About the Author

John Hutchins was born in Plymouth, Devon where he now continues to live. Having originally studied for a degree in drama and public media at Trinity and All Saints College, Leeds, he has spent most of his working life on local newspapers in Devon and Cornwall.

John now works as a reporter and sub-editor on the *Tavistock Times Gazette,* previously being employed in a similar post at the *Falmouth Packet* and *South West Farmer*. He has also been a reporter for the *West Briton* in Truro, *The Sunday Independent* in Plymouth and an editorial assistant on *Housebuyer* magazine in Teddington, Middlesex.

John's first published book *The Carved Angel*, tells the story of Tommy Wagstaff's First World War experiences, and it is from this book that the lovable character of *Our Patch* evolved.

Contents

Introduction
&
Acknowledgements

I thought readers of this book may like to know how the idea of *Our Patch* was conceived – an interesting tale (tail) in itself.

At the launch of my first book, *The Carved Angel,* which was held at The Plymouth Athenaeum in October 2014, I received a totally unexpected and wonderful gift from my friend and work colleague at the *Tavistock Times*, Lindsay Turpin; she and a friend had baked a cake with the cover of *The Carved Angel* cleverly decorated on the top of it. It was such a unique and thoughtful gesture I wondered how to repay her. Knowing that she and my fellow editorial colleagues were devoted to their cats and dogs I wrote a few fictional pages creating a family pet for Tommy Wagstaff, the 'hero' of the saga, which is set in a fictional coal mining village in North Yorkshire just before, during and after the First World War.

I had to think what sort of dog breed would a working class miner's family possess – perhaps a greyhound or a whippet or even a Jack Russell – all popular with the colliery community at the time – the first two for their racing (and gambling) opportunities and the latter for ratting or other bloodthirsty 'sport'. In the end I decided on a dog I only knew vaguely through its connection with a well-known North Eastern amateur football team with mining roots – the Bedlington Terriers.

I soon discovered that Bedlington terriers are intelligent and friendly companions, have good hunting instincts and a distinctive machine-gun bark with an unusual sheep-like appearance. Despite their modest size they are noted for their stubbornness – not backing down if threatened, even by other dogs physically larger.

With a cocky (not spaniel) attitude and a belief in his own superiority to both 'four paws' (other animals) and most 'two paws' (humans in his doggy language), 'Our Patch' was introduced into the Wagstaff pack.

There are many 'acknowledgements' to be made: the first to a terrific Collie cross called Ben, who was our family pet for 17 years, and provided the source of inspiration for the chapter dedicated to the raid of Mr Fishwicks' butcher's shop. This was based on Ben's own exploits at a butcher's shop in West Park in Plymouth, leaving me highly embarrassed as his owner while he enjoyed the ill-gotten loot of a string of sausages.

Thank you so much to Malcolm Sheppard and his family of United Writers in Cornwall for their professionalism (and Malcolm's patience) in their production of this beautifully laid out book.

Many thanks are also given to the talented Cornish artist

Carol Rea for her splendid and imaginative drawings which grace the pages to illustrate the story. By coincidence (or perhaps by design of the Great Bedlington In The Sky), Carol has been a Bedlington terrier owner herself and has breathed life into *Our Patch* with her drawings. My gratitude also to Jane Andrew, the illustrator of *The Carved Angel*, for wisely recommending Carol.

Thank you to all my fellow members of the Plymouth Athenaeum Writers' Group who had to 'endure' listening to my reading early drafts of Patch's adventures and also for their constructive comments.

Thanks also to fellow United Writers' author and colleague at the *Tavistock Times* Ted Sherrell, for his valued advice and friendship, and to Sue Hunt, a fellow member of St Francis Church in Honicknowle, Plymouth for her much appreciated faith and encouragement in this book.

However, the biggest thank you of all is to the person who has inspired me all my life and of whom I owe the biggest debt of gratitude – my beloved mother Doris Hutchins. Mum was the first reader (and critic) of *Our Patch* but sadly she passed away before the book was published. I will be forever grateful to her for her endless love and the joy she gave me from the many fond memories we shared.

Finally, I do hope you enjoy the many escapades of *Our Patch* and join him and his friends (and enemies) again in his next adventure *Our Patch to The Rescue*.

John Hutchins

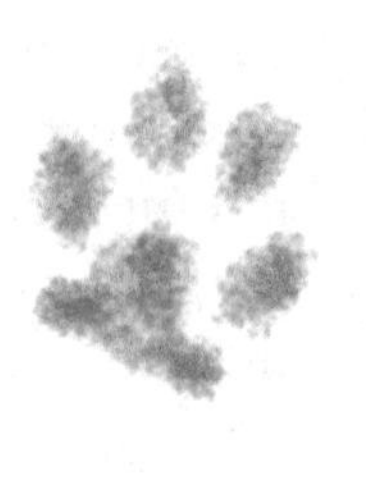

1

Puppy Dog Eyes

'OW many times I got to tell yer, our Tommy, yer can't 'ave a dog lad,' said Da Wagstaff. 'I understand, it's only natural, but it's 'ard enuff to put food on table for the six of us and it's not fair on yer Ma.'

If ever a 'hound dog' expression applied to a human being then no better example could have come from the face of eleven-year-old Tommy Wagstaff than at that moment.

'I know Da, but...' Tommy's voice began to choke with disappointment but he respected what his father had told him.

Da was right of course, he reasoned, and it would not be fair on Ma, who had enough to do without having a dog under her feet all day and cleaning up after it. Tommy turned on his heels towards the front door with his head down and 'his tail between his legs'. He spun around again, hoping for one last appeal to convince his parents and, in particular, his Ma – who he stared at and silently implored with 'puppy-dog eyes' – hoping that if he could sway her, then surely Da would soon follow her lead.

'But Joe Kirk has a Jack Russell cross, Growler. 'E's a good ratter and they never 'ave any vermin trouble in their house or 'ave to worry about his Da's pigeons,' Tommy informed his parents. This plea was his trump card, as Tommy knew that Da's pigeons were his pride and joy – apart from Ma and the children, of course – but his admonitions fell on deaf ears.

'Sorry son,' replied Da. 'What d'yer want me to do? Pay for a dog and feed it or not make yer Ma and little Emma go to bed 'ungry lad?'

Tommy had no answer to that and there was no further debate – although he didn't mind that much if his brothers Edward and Victor went to bed hungry!

As soon as he was out of the front door Da and Ma laughed out loud.

'Eh, Florrie love. Did yer see his little face? The last time I saw it like that was when 'e 'eard that Aston Villa had beaten Newcastle United in the FA Cup final,' joked Da.

Ma smiled before adding, 'Yer shouldn't tease 'im so Joe.'

Two weeks later, on Tommy's twelfth birthday, the eldest 'bairn' of the Wagstaff family came hurtling through the door, eager to be home and out of school and even more eager to go outside with his brothers to 'ave a kick-around with their pigskin bladder of a ball. He glanced longingly down at the contents on the kitchen table; Tommy looked at Ma, who nodded, and he quickly grabbed one of her freshly cooked jam tarts that she had been preparing lovingly for the family that afternoon.

Tommy was about to turn to go out the door again but even in his haste he noticed there was a strange atmosphere in the air; he could not quite comprehend the total silence emanating from the rest of the Wagstaff household. Victor, Edward and little Emma – along with Ma – had suddenly stopped what they were doing at the entry of their brother and all immediately looked towards him – more baffling for Tommy was that they all had big grins on their faces – as 'wide as the Wear' as Da would often say. His 'little sis' tugged at her mother's apron and tip toed to cup her hands and whisper something in Ma's ear before bursting into a giggle. Ma smiled and put her finger to her grinning lips to instruct her daughter 'not to say anymore'.

'Where's Da?' queried a suspicious Tommy, ''e's finished his shift, hasn't 'e?'

At that moment Da lifted the latch of the door and walked in, slightly stooped and tightly holding the two sides of his only coat together with his hands, as if coming in from the a bitter north easterly gale force wind.

'By 'eck, Tommy lad, it's cold out there,' exclaimed Da.

Everybody burst out laughing, except Tommy who was puzzled by his Da's strange behaviour. He couldn't understand why his father was so cold. It was the middle of June and it was a beautiful, sunny day.

'Had Da caught a chill or something?' he reasoned and immediately began to worry. Then all was 'revealed', for from under the jacket that Da was pretending to hug for warmth he produced, in a way that any professional magician would have been proud of, a little trembling bundle of white fur with distinctive liver spots.

Tommy stood there, wide-eyed and completely lost for words, as Pa handed over a yelping, wriggling ball of canine energy, clawing the air with his tiny paws and demanding attention from the surrounding Wagstaffs.

'Oh Da,' croaked Tommy, hardly able to form the words, ''E's just grand!'

Emma could hardly contain her excitement before confiding to her big brother, 'Da traded 'im for Pegasus.'

Tommy was open-mouthed and incredulous at this piece of news.

'Da, Ma… I can't…' Tommy's voice almost broke down with emotion knowing his father had sacrificed his prize homing pigeon to purchase the puppy.

'Don't say anythin' lad,' interrupted Da, raising his hand up to Tommy to stop his boy from uttering another word. 'All I want to hear from you, Tommy lad, is that yer look after 'im and exercise 'im properly. 'If yer don't,' said Pa, who put on his stern look and wagged his finger to underline the point he was making, 'If yer don't lad, I'm sure I can find room for another champion pigeon instead.'

Da had a wry grin as he spelt out his warning because he knew that there was not 'a cat in hell's chance' of that happening.

'Course I will, Da,' assured an ecstatic Tommy, before he scooped up the little dog and held him in the air in triumph; as if he was lifting the FA Cup itself at the end of the final, as the winning captain of the Newcastle United team, and showing the gleaming trophy off to an appreciative crowd.

'This is the best day ever,' stuttered an exuberant and emotional Tommy, and all the Wagstaff clan laughed as they shared his joy and welcomed the newest addition to their family.

'The best day ever,' he repeated, to everyone's amusement.

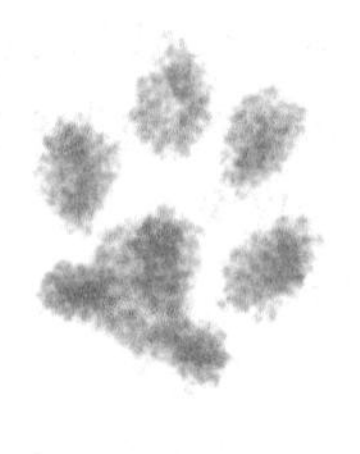

2

This is My Patch

IN the next few weeks, as the Wagstaffs adapted to the latest arrival to their family and, perhaps more importantly, the little puppy got used to them, there were some lively 'debates' in the household on what exactly to call their four-legged friend.

''Ow about Rover?' offered nine-year-old Edward, eager to state his opinion and who, in truth, had only one name in his mind.

'No, not Rover,' implored eight-year-old Emma, 'I don't want to lose him… ever,' and her little eyes welled with tears at the possibility.

'What about Fluffy?' she enthused, as her tears suddenly evaporated as quickly as they came; Emma put her little hand down to stroke the object of her worship…

'Look at his beautiful coat of fur, it's so soft and fluffy. I think it's a grand name.'

It was true, the puppy indeed possessed a white, shiny, lustrous coat with an almost fleece-like quality whose background was dominated by a few patches of sandy, liver-coloured spots matching the colour of his nose – which only added to his distinction. This was topped off by a prominent square tuft at the top of his head, a trait specific to the breed.

Such was Emma's determination to name the little dog that she took a few steps across the room before turning around, going down on her haunches, holding out her loving arms and attempting to call him over.

'Here Fluffy, come on boy,' she cooed, 'come to Emma.'

But 'Fluffy' didn't move.

The puppy looked at little Emma with a puzzled, and somewhat nervous, expression on its cute, young face.

'Rover's bad enough,' it thought, 'but there's no way I'm going to be a Fluffy. No self-respecting Bedlington terrier like me is going to demean itself by answering to a ludicrous name like that!

'The dogs in our family for generations have been given noble, doggy names like Bosun, Hunter or indeed, my personal favourite, Rebel. But 'Fluffy'? Never! – and the little puppy's face sank between its paws before its young throat let off a short whine at the prospect of such a nomenclature being assigned to him for the rest of his life.

Emma persisted, determined that although the youngest and 'just a girl' in the eyes of her three brothers, she would have a part in the important task of naming the family pet.

'Well, if not Fluffy, what about Archie? It's a lovely name for a dog,' pleaded Emma enthusiastically.

At the mere mention of the word 'Archie' the little terrier gave a louder whine and retreated slowly backwards, away from Emma, with his four paws. Victor and Edward laughed at his reaction.

''E won't be called Archie,' scoffed Edward, 'and I can't say I blame 'im. It's too lah-de-dah for any dog around 'ere.'

Emma frowned, knowing her suggestions were being ignored.

''Ow' about Trapper?' piped up Victor enthusiastically, who had waited until Emma's humiliating rejection by the animal to make his claim.

Victor clearly had visions of 'borrowing' the animal from his big brother so he could 'teach' it to go ratting – anticipating a bloody dual between the little dog and a giant rat.

'No,' screamed Emma, horrified that such a small, innocent, beautiful creature should be initiated into the brutal art of ratting – even though she really had no idea what it exactly was.

''E's just a puppy, leave him alone,' she cried, and she punched Victor in the arm to emphasise her dissatisfaction.

'All right, all right, little sis,' responded Victor, in mock surrender and ignoring her punch. 'Trapper's got a bit of growin' up to do before 'e takes on those big colliery rats.'

He then, to Emma's dismay, protruded his teeth into a rat-like snarl before grabbing his sister's arm and, leaning over, playfully pretending to bite her shoulder.

'Stop it, Victor,' she wailed, but Victor just laughed and went in for another bite.

'Leave yer little sis' alone,' commanded the eldest Wagstaff bairn.

'And as fer namin' the dog, that's for me to decide, nobody else. 'E's my dog and I'll call 'im what I like.'

This sudden outburst from Tommy left his brothers and sisters in no doubt who was going to name the puppy and no more was said again on the subject between the siblings.

A few days later the children were in 'the Patch' as they

called the family allotment and the young terrier decided to join them.

As usual Da was in charge of proceedings, turning over the soil and removing the weeds.

'What yer reckon, our Emma,' said Da. 'What if we put in a little rhubarb plant or two? Yer like yer rhubarb pie, don't yer, lass?' grinned Da, knowing the answer before he even asked the question.

'Oh, yes please Da,' she replied, 'and 'opefully Ma will let me help her bake it.'

'I'm sure she will, pet. I'm sure she will,' Da beamed.

'And we will 'elp yer eat it, Emma,' declared Edward, much to his sister's obvious annoyance.

Da smiled, before unfurling a small sack to reveal four healthy bulbs of rhubarb ready to be planted.

'Now come on, Tommy. You dig a couple of holes and I'll dig the other two,' said Da.

While father and son were busy with their spades digging away, the little puppy, much to the astonishment of all around him, jumped in the space between Tommy and Da, and with his paws started to dig away frantically to create a hole of his own. The puppy's efforts only resulted in soil being scattered all over – especially directly behind him – to the amusement of the children and the bewilderment of Da.

When the puppy had noticed that 'Master Da' and 'Young Master Tommy' (as he began to call them) had stopped their digging, the little dog turned around to see why they had given up on this fun game. As he did, all the Wagstaffs laughed at the sight of the little fellow with his liver-covered nose covered in mud. To add to the merriment the puppy shook himself and sneezed in an attempt to unblock the bits of northern soil which had made their way up his nostrils.

'Eh,' said Edward, ''e likes our patch.'

'Aye,' agreed Tommy, with a big grin on his face. 'And that's what I'm going to call the little fellow. 'E's Our Patch.'

Everybody laughed and nodded in agreement at the naming of the latest member of the Wagstaff family.

Even 'Patch' approved because he knew instinctively that, as a Bedlington terrier, there was not a dog in Hillthorpe who could possibly be 'a Patch' on him.

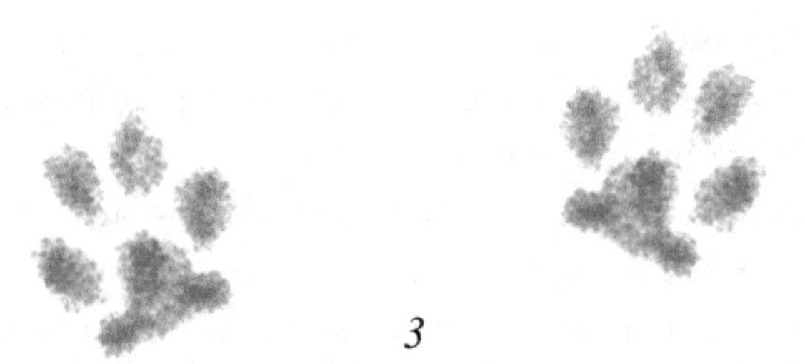

3

Top of the Class

FROM the time of, in Tommy's words, 'the best day ever' when he had held the little puppy in the air with triumph, both boy and dog were inseparable. There grew a special bond between them and both took the simple pleasure in the delight of being in each other's company. For hours each day, after Tommy had finished school, they would explore Hillthorpe and its surrounding countryside.

Although to the puppy Da was obviously master and 'top dog' of the house, it was to Young Master Tommy that his loyalty and affection lay.

Edward and Victor were, to Patch, fellow members of the Wagstaff litter, vying for attention; he enjoyed nothing better than being outside with the two boys 'playing' their daily kick about and getting under their feet, chasing the ball and butting it with his forehead – although he soon learned that sinking his teeth into the spherical object was a 'sending off' (and home) offence which resulted in a temporary ban and was not a good idea if he wanted to continue joining in their fun.

As for the lovely Emma – well what was there for a young

dog not to like! Her natural abundance of love and affection, especially the way she always gave him a big hug and kiss on the forehead when she met him from school, soon had Patch eating out of her paw.

Of course, being an intelligent dog – and naturally Bedlington terriers had this in abundance compared to lesser canines – when it came to food and drink Patch soon learned that if he wanted to keep his stomach well lined then it was Mistress Ma to whom he had to make an alliance. For her alone he reserved his most pitiful looks, as if the next morsel of food she handed down to him would be the only thing fending off his death by starvation – but only just. It worked every time.

Whenever Ma was in the kitchen preparing the next meal for the family, Patch would be sat on top of the chair opposite her, next to the table. While she went about her cooking, he would be looking up at her with adoring, beseeching eyes. Of course, apart from the occasional whimper – or was that a hunger pang? – Patch sat and waited with the patience of the most pious saint.

Eventually, of course, Ma would relent and throw the odd piece of skirt in his direction if she was making a stew, or a broken biscuit freshly out of the oven.

'Aweh with yer, Patch,' she would cry, with a warm smile on her face, knowing exactly what the puppy was after. 'There be no more 'til supper time boy.'

With his latest spoils quickly bolted down his gullet Patch knew it was time to leave while he was winning and so he scratched the door to be let out, to which Ma duly obliged.

'Same time tomorrow, Mistress,' thought Patch, as he left Ma to her chores and he left to his new adventures.

Every week day, except on school holidays, Patch, without fail, waited patiently, rain or shine, snow or gale, outside the gate of Hillthorpe Elementary at 3pm sharp – waiting for the pupils of the two school classes to come bursting out of its doors.

Tommy's class mate Wally Smethick told his pal that he reckoned that the dog's timing was so impeccable that ' 'e must be a watchdog, and a Swiss one at that!'

It was the same in the mornings when Patch would accompany his Young Master, and the rest of the Wagstaff children, to answer the clanging of the school bell rung by Miss Tucker, the nursery teacher. After Tommy had given Patch a pat on the head followed by Emma giving him a gentle kiss on the nose, the three reluctant boys, accompanied by a more enthusiastic 'little Sis', forlornly made their way inside the school gate.

The young terrier waited until the doors closed and the school day began. Patch would then give a little whimper, having lost his playmate, and then turn to seek new entertainment for the day elsewhere.

One autumn day at 3pm after watching all the other pupils come streaming out eagerly from the school door, many to be greeted by their mothers, Patch waited patiently for his Young Master to appear – but much to the little dog's bewilderment, a further ten minutes passed and there was still no sign of Tommy.

Even Victor and Edward ran past the little dog in their haste, although little Emma stopped to give him his customary hug before telling Patch 'that Tommy won't be long, pet' before she skipped off to find her home and Ma.

So Patch went through the school gate and towards the

classroom door, which, by good fortune, was slightly ajar. The little dog pushed the bottom of the wooden frame with his paw and entered – unbeknown to his Young Master and Mr Neilsen the schoolmaster, who were inside.

'Now Wagstaff, here's a clean cloth. I want you to wipe down all the desks and chairs before you go, empty the bins and wipe the blackboard. Don't forget the inkwells. Is that clear boy?'

Tommy nodded.

'Haven't you got a tongue in your head, boy?' scowled Mr Neilsen.

'Yes sir,' replied Tommy.

'I hope you have learned your lesson today, Wagstaff.'

'Yes, sir,' responded Tommy once more, whose true thoughts revealed that when it came to 'lessons' there was not much that Mr Neilsen could ever teach him.

Patch sat down on his haunches sensing that Young Master would be some time yet.

'I shall be back in 15 minutes and I want this classroom spick and span Wagstaff,' said the teacher, and with that he marched off to his office, as he liked to call the only other private room in the building, and slammed the door behind him.

Tommy bent down and with his cloth began to rub the nearest desk, before he eyed Patch and grinned.

Patch jumped up and put his paws on Young Master's knees and his tail wagged excitedly.

'Down Patch lad,' Tommy said in a lowered tone. 'Just go outside for a while. I won't be long, there's a good dog. I don't want Nasty Neilsen finding you 'ere boy. With that he began to shoo Patch out in the direction of the front door before continuing his task of cleaning the desks, one that he was anxious to finish.

But Patch, being a stubborn dog – a well know Bedlington trait – did not want to go outside, particularly as he had noticed through the window it was beginning to rain heavily, so reasoned the shelter of the classroom was better than being out. He decided to hang around but his attention was taken by the blackboard and two white squiggly marks in particular.

Patch sat immediately in the centre front of the board and his gaze transferred from one squiggly mark to the other – and back again.

Tommy could not help but notice this unusual sight and went over to investigate what Patch was up to.

He looked up at the blackboard and on it were two words, both written in capital letters and left by Miss Tucker from the elementary class – one said DOG, the other CAT.

Tommy looked down at Patch and could not help but notice how the little dog appeared to be studying each word.

'Well boy, that one there says DOG, so that's why you must be so interested. I never knew dogs could read,' joked Tommy.

'Of course I can read, Young Master,' an irritated Patch thought to himself. 'I'm a Bedlington terrier, I'm not stupid!'

So Patch thought, and being of an inquisitiveness nature and an enquiring mind, dwelled upon the words DOG and CAT.

Suddenly Patch was hit by a revelation, and one that confirmed his innermost thoughts.

'Of course, DOG spells GOD backwards. It all makes sense. If, indeed there is a superior being who created all the universe then indeed a dog must be at the centre of it. It wouldn't surprise me if GOD was a Bedlington terrier.'

Patch was certainly satisfied at his logical conclusion as his stare lingered on the word DOG.

He then transferred his focus onto the word CAT, which he soon reasoned was TAC backwards.

'Says it all,' he thought, 'cats are such useless, frivolous creatures.'

Just at the moment the 'office' door began to open, Patch had the good sense to run out of the classroom before he got his Young Master into any more trouble; he waited outside for him in the rain.

While he passed the time before Tommy joined him, Patch contemplated and thought a little more on his recent discovery.

'If GOD is a dog then why did he create CATS?'

He concluded that this enigma obviously needed further thought!

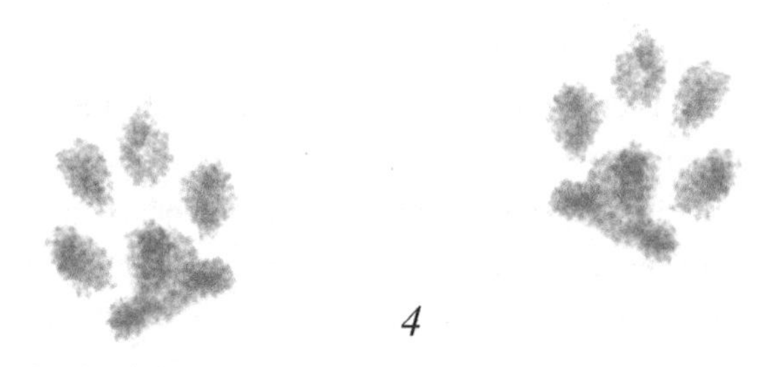

4

Angelic Encounter

AS Tommy grew into his teenage years so did his little puppy into an energetic and playful young dog. Wherever young Tommy Wagstaff went so did his Patch, and they came such a common sight together that if on the odd occasion the boy was walking the streets of Hillthorpe by himself he would be often asked by a friendly villager: 'Where's thy Patch then, lad?'

It was the same for the dog; if he was trotting by himself on his adventures folk would ask: 'Where's yer Young Master today then, boy?'

At the age of 14, Tommy left Hillthorpe Elementary to take up employment in the colliery, helping to grade the coal in the sorting shed they called 'the screens'.

The evening before his Young Master started work Patch was at the special 'ceremony' when Tommy was presented with a little piece of wood, in the shape of what he heard called a 'carved angel' – or Saint Barbara, the patron saint of miners. It was whittled by Master 'to protect Young Master down the mine'.

Patch was most intrigued; many a night he sat by Da's side

next to the fire while he worked on the stick and could not wait to get his teeth into it for a chew but, in the end, he decided to let his Young Master have it, if that was his Master's intention.

'There were plenty more sticks around to chew!' he thought.

But something strange happened at the time when Tommy was being presented with his new stick by Master and Mistress. Although it was dark, and there was only the light from the hearth fire and a weak glow from an oil lamp; suddenly the whole room was bathed in the most radiant light. Patch looked up and saw this most beautiful lady with long, red hair 'floating' above Young Master, Mistress Ma and little Mistress Emma. She had great big white feathered wings, and at first Patch thought it could be a great big turkey, like the ones he had seen when he and Young Master had passed a nearby farm on their many walks. But no, the beautiful figure looked down at Patch and beamed and the little dog felt the warm, loved feeling he had whenever Mistress Emma had given him a big hug – only this was even better!

'And boy, did she smell nice!' thought Patch.

He barked in his excitement but his Master told him to be quiet which only frustrated the little dog even more.

'Why can they not see what I do?' wondered Patch. 'They must know how bright it is in here? Why can't the rest of the pack see the beautiful lady with the big wings?'

As long as he lived it was a mystery that Patch could never work out.

'Even a Bedlington doesn't have all the answers,' he concluded, before adding: 'Obviously as a Bedlington my sight is far superior to any human as are all of my other senses.'

The next morning Tommy was due to start his shift at 5.50am, but even this early start was not enough to put off Patch. Just like when he would accompany the Wagstaff children to school, so Patch would go with his Young Master to his new work place. No matter how dark, or cold or bitter the early mornings, Patch would leave the warmth and comfort of his basket and his beloved blanket and follow Tommy out of the door. He escorted his Young Master to his workplace and more often than not he would be given a friendly rub on the head from one or two of the miners or a hug from one of the screen girls – or better still to Patch, half a biscuit from one of his many admirers.

Then his Young Master would stroke him on the head before disappearing into the screen, and as soon as Tommy was out of sight the little dog would make his way home and scratch at the door to be let in by Ma. Patch would then return to his blanket for some more kip as Ma prepared breakfast for the rest of the Wagstaff children as they got ready for school – while the little dog waited to do his next escort duty.

Although Patch enjoyed many an adventure during the day whilst his Young Master was down at the colliery, at 2.59pm sharp, wherever he was and whatever he was up to, Patch never failed to get to the gates of the sorting shed before the pit hooter announced the end of Tommy's shift. No matter how hard, or dirty or boring his work had been that day the sight of his loving dog waiting patiently to greet him always produced a big grin on Tommy's face.

'Aweh, lad, it's Our Patch,' he would say every time as if he was surprised to see him and the little terrier would jump up on his Young Master and wag his tail in delight at the return of his favourite playmate.

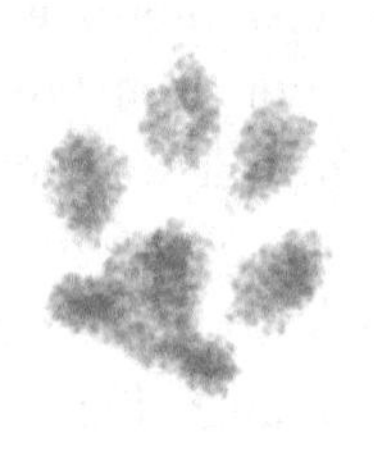

5

Archie Enemy

ONE fine summer's day Patch was taking his Young Master for a spot of exercise around the village. He had let Tommy off the leash because Patch thought it was not fair on the lad to be hampered by such barbaric constraints.

As they made their way up the cobbled street Patch decided to pay a 'courtesy call' to the home of his 'Archie enemy' as he liked to call him – a 'working' (so called) cocker spaniel called Archie. By coincidence Patch often heard his Young Master speak in poor terms of some young fellow at the mine called Archie Tilsley.

'Perhaps all Archies are nasty bits of work,' pondered Patch, whose thoughts turned to the vicious little mutt who, in his mind, was a disgrace to the collective noun of the word 'dog'.

'There's no dog worse than a yapper,' thought Patch, 'and boy, is that dog a yapper!'

As Tommy gathered pace in anticipation of whatever Ma was about to serve at her table for his tea, Patch veered toward number one, Moor View – one of the few semi-detached houses in the village in contrast to the rows of miners' terraced cottages, and even rarer, one with its own walled garden with gate; a fact that Mrs Curtois-Pughs, the wife of its owner, was extremely proud of – just as she was of her own double-barrelled name – and there was not a woman in the village who had not been reminded of the fact, mostly by Mrs Curtois-Pughs herself.

Her husband was the chief clerk at Hillthorpe Colliery – a white collar position which, in his wife's view, was of far superior social standing to most people in the village.

Of course, Mrs Curtois-Pughs had conveniently long forgotten that she herself was formerly Ethel Bigglesthwaite, a collier's daughter from Daleswick in the neighbouring village, who had caught the eye of a junior clerk at the colliery when she worked in the screens. Now married, she certainly considered herself superior to most folk in the village – as did her much pampered pet dog. Like his mistress, Archie enjoyed life's material comforts and considered himself of a higher social rank than those around him – especially compared to all the other dogs in the village who, to him, were just vulgar 'scruffs'.

His abundant good looks Archie took for granted; his glossy coat and remarkable long ears that flapped when he deigned to run, just added to his natural cuteness. Of course, he had his mistress wrapped around his dainty paw; one whimper and she was immediately by his side.

If there was one thing that Archie hated it was other dogs in his garden; any other dog that could possibly catch the eye of his mistress was to him a threat and he protected his privileged position with a vengeance.

As Patch approached the house he noticed Mrs Curtois-Pughs outside sitting at a garden table enjoying the summer's day, busy with her crochet. She was accompanied by self-confessed village 'dragon' – a short, rotund lady, aged in her mid-sixties – the indomitable Mrs Prudence Popplethwaite. Whatever had happened to her husband was one of the village's hotly disputed and unsolved mysteries. She had magnanimously joined her fellow 'tabby' for their weekly sewing session, china tea and catch-up of the latest gossip.

Through the gates Patch observed his nemesis Archie lying prostrate on the chair opposite, catching the warm rays of the sun with his head comfortably resting on a floral designed, plumped up, velvet cushion.

The words 'stitch and bitch' flashed through Patch's mind. 'Stitch and bitch,' – including 'that insult to doghood, that wimp Archie Curtois-Pughs' in his description.

'Isn't my little Archie so well behaved, Mrs Popplethwaite? And so adorable,' cooed the hostess.

'He's a credit to his breed, Mrs Curtois-Pughs', replied Mrs Popplethwaite almost swooning, eager to impress one of the few fellow 'refined genteel ladies' in her social circle.

She added, to curry even more favour: 'I'm sure Archie, with his pedigree, will win the 'Dog of the Year' trophy at this year's Hillthorpe and Daleswick Summer Fete. He's such a darling little chap.'

Mrs Curtois-Pughs beamed with pride at the thought of 'the Dog of the Year' trophy on her mantelpiece, or even better still on a specially bespoke table to display it in the front window. She put down her crochet and selected a chocolate truffle from a bowl on the table. Mrs Curtois-Pughs looked across adoringly to her beloved pet, who began to open its mouth in anticipation of a tasty treat.

'You have been such a good boy, Archie dearest,' purred

his mistress. 'I think my little baby deserves a treat, yes you do,' and with that she began to lean over to Archie to give him the sweet when the intended recipient noticed Patch looking through the bars of the gate.

Immediately Archie barrel-rolled over and jumped down from the chair, causing his mistress to drop her truffle on the floor along with a full cup of tea which went flying across the lap of their 'illustrious' guest.

Mrs Popplethwaite screamed, feeling the liquid dribble down her latest dress, which she had especially commissioned for her 'audience' with her esteemed hostess.

The cocker spaniel dashed for the gate, all his fur flying, hackles up, his long ears desperately attempting to catch up with the rest of his body. Archie, knowing very well there was a sturdy iron gate between him and his perceived intruder, let out the most vicious, threatening bark that he could muster – although for those witnessing the scene it came out more as a cross between a splutter and a squeak.

Patch was affronted by this most unwelcoming of canine greetings and responded with what he would describe as one of his best 'Bedlington Roars' – such was its volume and velocity, combined with its clear intention of threat, that the unfortunate recipient of its percussion instantly retreated, at full speed, behind the folds of his mistress's skirt, and started to make whimpering noises as if he had been trodden on by a passing elephant.

The distressed Mrs Curtois-Pughs was in total shock and cried: 'Oh my poor baby Archie, what has that nasty mongrel done to you, my precious?'

'Mongrel?' thought a clearly affronted Patch. 'I'm not a mongrel, lady, I am a pedigree Bedlington terrier. How dare you?' and he barked again at this latest indignation, which only made the quivering Archie even more stressed and insecure.

'How dare that nasty, vicious brute of an animal attack my poor, innocent little Archie,' an affronted Mrs Curtois-Pughs reproached Tommy. 'Your dog is an absolute menace. It should be kept on a lead. It's completely out of control.'

'No 'e's not Mrs,' replied Tommy. 'Patch is a good dog. It was your Archie who started it. 'E attacked Our Patch.'

'You tell her, Young Master,' thought Patch indignantly. 'Open the gate, Mrs, and let me at that pampered excuse for a dog.'

'How dare you talk to me like that Tommy Wagstaff,' snapped Archie's mistress. 'Don't you know who you are talking to?'

'I saw it all Master Wagstaff. Your nasty cur deliberately went to attack that sweet, little angel Archie, who was just protecting his mistress,' gleefully added 'prime witness' Mrs Popplethwaite.

'I'm just telling it as it was, Mrs. Your dog started it,' replied Tommy in a firm but conciliatory tone.

Patch looked up in disgust at his arch enemy, who was now cosseted in the safety of his mistress's arms and peering down and snarling at the terrier, fangs showing.

'If you cannot control your dog, young man, I will report him to the village constable,' Tommy was informed by Mrs Curtois-Pughs.

Tommy said nowt, knowing that any response would be useless and besides, with his Da sick and struggling to hold down his job at the pit, the last thing Tommy wanted was to antagonise the wife of the colliery's chief clerk.

'Come on Patch lad, time te go 'ome. Ma will be waitin' fer us fer tea.'

Patch returned the glare of his adversary. If he wasn't mistaken, as the 'dreadful dragon' and Archie's mistress petted and fussed over their 'little baby' he could swear that the pitiful excuse of a canine had stuck out his tongue at him as a parting shot – a most undoggedly action, in his book.

Patch snorted with indignation but just as he was about to follow his Young Master up the cobbled street he raised and cocked his right back leg and left his 'calling card' which proceeded to drip down the side of the iron gate – much to the chagrin and disgust of Mrs Curtois-Pughs and her pampered pooch – and the secret amusement of Mrs Prudence Popplethwaite.

6

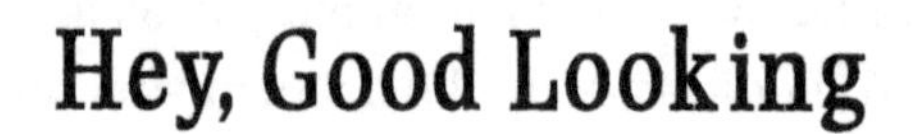

Hey, Good Looking

THERE was a sharp nip in the air that autumn day but the sun still beamed down on the North Yorkshire pit village. Clear and crisp, it was 'a fine day' as Da would say – but to a man who had spent most of his working life 300 feet down a coal shaft, any day on the surface was 'a fine day'.

The two pals, Tommy and Patch, were on their regular 'patrol' one Tuesday afternoon after the former had finished his shift for the day in the screens.

They were going 'nowhere in particular', just out for a stroll, but Patch did not mind – there was always, to the inquisitive young terrier, 'another adventure around the next corner.'

Indeed, as they turned into Victoria Street, the main road in the village and the venue for a handful of shops and trades, Young Master and Patch were about to pass Hardwick's Ironmongery when a certain object caught the terrier's eye.

Perhaps it was the glimpse of the sunlight that reflected off the shiny object but the young dog decided it needed further investigation.

'Come on, Patch. There's nowt 'ere for you boy,' said

Tommy, and indeed to the human eye there wasn't – just an assortment of ironmongery placed outside the shop front on display – a tin bath, a second hand Singer sewing machine, a brass bedstead, a coal scuttle and a few other objects for sale. However, Patch, with his superior 'doggy vision' and instincts, had found something that just took his breath away.

Enclosed in a gilded frame and standing almost half the height as his Young Master was a gleaming, shiny window and in that glass what he beheld just rooted the little terrier to the spot. For there, standing just a couple of feet away from him, was the most beautiful creature he had ever seen in his life. Although young Patch was perhaps not familiar with the term 'love at first sight' before – now he was. It hit him like the feeling he had when he first saw a string of sausages hanging up in the village butchers as a puppy.

Patch gazed at the dog before him and could not help but be drawn into its almond coloured eyes, which were small but of such evident intelligence that they hinted possession of a deep knowledge beyond this world itself; it was as if Patch sensed that the vision before him knew everything about him and had such power and beauty that it threatened to suck in his very soul itself.

Patch was completely barkless, for once in his life, and stood stiff and erect as if frozen to the spot.

'Who is this dog before me?' he thought with heart pounding. 'Why, I know of every hound in the village and even every cat unfortunately, but I have never laid eyes on such a dog before at the ironmongery! Especially not one such as this exquisite creature standing before me.'

Patch was smitten.

He cautiously went towards the little dog before him, or

was it a vision? Bedlingtons were renowned for their courage and in the best tradition of the breed he put his best, and only, nose forward. But as he did so, so did the object of his curiosity, until their noses both touched. Surprisingly to Patch, the most sensitive part of his anatomy did not feel doggy nose against doggy nose – no, he just felt a little bump; even more curiously, when Patch withdrew slightly – so did the other dog – after the initial contact a little cloud of steam appeared on the window at the spot where they touched.

'Oh my Dog?' thought Patch. 'How odd!'

Patch then barked at the dog with one of his best 'Bedlington Roars', but unnervingly for him, although he definitely heard the sound of his own voice, when the other dog looked as if it barked at the same time, no noise emanated from the handsome stranger.

So then Patch shook his head in disbelief and the other dog followed suit. Patch was beginning to get really agitated now at these weird goings on and twisted around for reassurance that his Young Master was still there – thankfully he was, but even he was looking at him with a great big grin on his face.

A bewildered Patch turned around again and again but the ironmonger's dog returned his stare. The more Patch glared, so did the other dog. So Patch tried a new tactic and lifted a left paw in salute to his new canine acquaintance and remarkably the little dog in front of him responded with his right paw. This was followed by Patch putting down his left paw and lifting his right paw in salute, and the other dog replied by putting down his right paw and raising his left paw.

Patch could not believe it! He tilted his head to the right in puzzlement only for the other dog to tilt his left, complete with an equally mystified expression.

'That dog is a handsome brute, no doubt about it,' thought Patch, 'but I've never met a dafter one. There's definitely something very odd about that dog!' he concluded. 'Unless it's making fun of me?'

So he did what any self-respecting Bedlington would do in the situation and barked again to make his frustration apparent to all around him. To his annoyance, so did the other dog, who appeared to bark but again no sound came out to match it.

Patch was getting really irked now and even thought about attacking the dog for ignoring his friendly advances.

'I hope for his sake his bite is worse than his bark,' snarled Patch to himself, whose initial 'love at first sight' had rapidly turned to anger.

'How rude,' thought Patch. 'He definitely can't be a Bedlington.'

'Come on, boy,' piped up Tommy, who was most entertained by Patch's encounter but wanted to be on his way, 'We can't be 'ere all day,' he told his furry friend.

With that a very confused Patch left the ironmonger's new dog and bid him farewell with a parting bark. There was no reply. Patch, though, had 'his final word' by leaving his calling card on the coal scuttle before scampering after Young Master who had already turned to go home.

For the next couple of days Patch gave the incident considerable thought, especially when lying in his basket with his head between his paws as the family settled down in the evening.

'Who was that dog at the ironmongery? Why did he find

him so attractive? It wasn't even a bitch! I'm a Bedlington terrier, 100 per cent dog, right down to the end of my tail,' thought a now worried Patch trying to reassure himself. 'A dog's dog!'

Such was his concern that Patch decided to avoid going past the ironmongery and let 'sleeping dogs lie'.

He wasn't avoiding a confrontation, he reasoned, 'Bedlingtons don't back down to any dog, no matter how big they are.'

'No, I'll make some enquiries tomorrow with the other dogs about the new handsome stranger in the village who can't bark and then I'll go back and pay him a visit.'

But as it happened, a few day's later – after Patch's investigations proved fruitless as the other dogs did not have a clue what he was woofing about – Tommy decided he wanted to go down Victoria Street. There was not much a reluctant Patch could do to persuade him otherwise.

'Come boy. What's the matter with yer? Get a move on,' coaxed Tommy to a dilatory Patch when they were approaching the ironmongery.

Much to Patch's amazement, this time there was no sign of the dog who had dominated his thoughts for the past few days.

He surveyed the scene, and outside the shop the same objects were displayed at the store front, all accept the gilded frame with the shiny window.

'Looks like Mr Hardwick has sold that mirror, boy,' exclaimed Tommy. Yer didn't 'alf 'ave a lot of fun looking into it the other day, Patch. I've never seen yer in such a state,' he added with a smile.

Patch eagerly looked around, pricked up his ears and

sniffed everywhere for a sign of the ironmonger's new dog but to no avail.

'My bark did it, that and my vicious glare. I've scared him off,' thought Patch. 'Don't mess with a Bedlington! Obviously that other dog got the message. This village ain't big enough for the two of us.'

Reassured in his 'doggyness' and with his pride restored, Patch swaggered with a newly found spring in his step behind Young Master, looking forward to his next adventure.

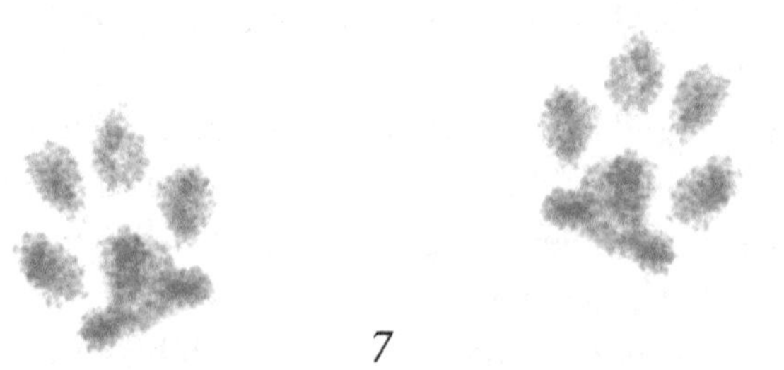

7

It's a Dog's Life

THERE were many pleasures in Patch's life which gave him a good deal of satisfaction. Of course, the terrier was the first to admit to himself, one of the major considerations to 'measure his pleasure' scale, was how empty, or more to the point, how full, his ever starving stomach was at any time.

Little pleasures included returning on a cold, frosty day to his basket – which was conveniently situated close enough to the fire to receive the benefits of its warmth – and snuggling up in his beloved blanket, especially if it was recently and lovingly washed and ironed by Mistress Ma.

Then there were the scraps off the table at meal times – Patch was constantly amazed how Tommy and Emma were particularly clumsy with their food, allowing it to drop on to the floor – often doing so just as Ma and Da's attention were elsewhere. The terrier felt it was his duty to scoop up the tasty treats; which he gleefully did – naturally, he reasoned – he was only helping out Mistress Ma and saving her work by keeping the floor clean.

Some comforts and treats were a constant in Patch's

world, such as playing 'headball' with the boys, rootin' and diggin' in the vegetable patch or going out 'on patrol' with the Young Master. Snoozing in the sun on top of Da's pigeon pen was another one, or sitting outside the baker's shop and inhaling the delicious aroma wafting from the ovens early in the morning – although he was disappointed that the one time a loaf fell off the handlebar of the baker boy's bike without the rider noticing and Patch dived on it and chewed off the crust – it tasted revolting. 'Ugh!' thought the dog, vowing never to dine on bread again.

Of course, then there was the best of all, what Patch liked to call 'Doggy heaven'! On a cold winter's evening there was nothing the little Bedlington loved more than being stretched out in front of the coal fire. The colder and more bitter it was outside, the more snug and smug Patch felt in the cosiest place in the cottage. It was the prime position and the rest of the Wagstaff pack fought for it but they all made way for the family pet – a spot that Emma had affectionately named 'Patch's place'.

Indeed it was Emma who added to his sensory delight. For basking in the warmth and glow from the fire Patch would, many a time, lie on his back prostrate, with three of his paws pointed directly in the air; he took this unusual, but vulnerable, exposed position, for his favourite part of the evening – 'Tic Time'.

As soon as Emma, or on a rare occasion Ma, called to Patch: 'Come on boy, it's 'Tic Time' he would roll on his back with three of his four paws stretched towards the ceiling, as if answering three of Mr Neilsen's questions to a Hillthorpe class at the same time.

Emma knelt down next to her pet, with an empty jam jar

placed at her side, and then proceeded to body search the young dog for any fleas or 'tics' residing in his fur. Any captured parasite would be deftly flicked off Emma's fingers into the jam jar. With the three paws erect to facilitate her efforts; his fourth fore left paw was held semi-cocked and limp, dangling in a pretence to 'fend off' the girl's advances as she foraged for fleas. It was a sight that brought much amusement to the Wagstaff family.

'He's definitely a southpaw,' offered Edward, commenting on Patch's antics.

'Well, he's definitely not a Boxer, he's a Bedlington,' added Victor, anxious to outdo his younger brother in the comic quips. Even Da laughed at that one.

Patch loved being the centre of attention from his fellow pack members and if that meant hamming it up to please his audience then he was more than happy to oblige. Suddenly one of Ma's ham bones flashed in front of Patch's mind but a flea running for its life across his navel quickly evaporated that brief image.

As Emma dived into his skin with her delicate fingers, Patch could hardly contain his satisfaction; his 'defence' paw offered scant resistance as she gently stroked his body surface in search of an unwanted parasite. At that moment, for Patch, basking in front of the open fire, there was not a place in Hillthorpe, or indeed the whole earth, where he would rather be. With a full stomach from one of Ma's stews, the prime position in front of the fire, surrounded by, and holding court, to the whole pack, and with the delightful Emma tickling his tummy – and 'boy, did she smell nice' – Patch was, indeed, in 'Doggy heaven!'

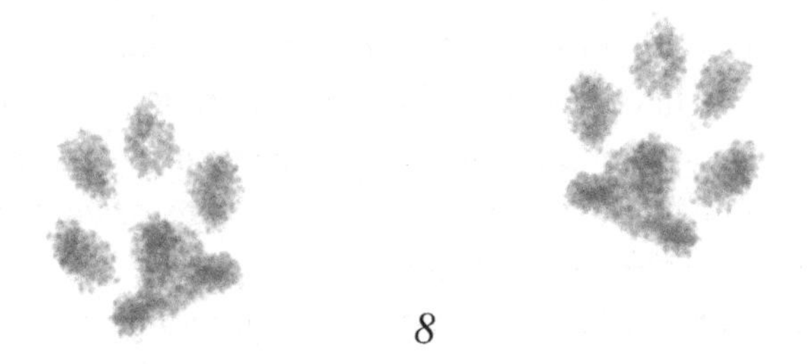

8

Did Someone Say Sausages?

EVERY new day brought about opportunities of fresh adventures for Patch, and the young dog was never disappointed when the evening came and he lay in his basket retracing his paw prints in his mind, recalling that day's events.

That particular day, and night, he was, as Pa put it, 'in the dog house' – not only with Mr Fishwick, the inappropriately named village butcher, but even worse, with Mistress Ma herself – for whom, Patch admitted to himself, it took some doing to raise her fur.

Strangely, though, Young Master seemed to be much amused, as were the rest of the Wagstaff siblings and even Da, by the predicament Patch had found himself in.

Being 'in the doghouse' with Mistress Ma had its consequences for the young terrier and one where it especially hurt him most of all – his stomach; in fact it was this part of his anatomy and his constant lookout to satiate his ravenous appetite, which had led Patch in the first place to all his present troubles.

As he lay still in his basket gazing at the dying embers of

the coal fire and began to shiver as the nip of the night chill began to have its effect, Patch buried his snout deeper into the refuge of his blanket; he whimpered to himself, and the self-pitying sound only helped to deaden the deafening rumbles from his stomach as his hunger pangs began to make their presence felt in sonic form.

'No. Mistress Ma has punished me very unfairly,' thought Patch, 'by not only taking away my rations this evening but also depriving me of my usual 'bonus' of scraps from the plates of Young Master Tommy and Young Mistress Emma.

'It's just not fair,' a desolate Patch reasoned to himself. 'A working dog like me is entitled to his rations – just like any miner. After all, I protect the family home, especially from the cats and rats, escort the young pups to school and Young Master to work in all weathers; help dig up their vegetable patch for them. . .'

Patch paused as at that moment he couldn't think of any more labours to add to the list, before concluding: 'And that's just to name a few!'

'No, all Mistress Ma has given me is a measly drop of water in my bowl and half a biscuit. Outrageous!'

With that, Patch sank deeper down in despair further into his blanket and grumbled to himself as his stomach rumbled for the umpteenth time that night.

'It's just not fair,' he mournfully repeated to himself, and with that the events of the day, which had led him to his present misfortune, began to unfold in his mind like a string of sausages being prepared in Mr Fishwick's butchery.

'Sausages,' Patch's ears pricked up at the very vision but his gut groaned again in response to these very succulent thoughts; knowing it was, alas, but just a dream and not about to become a reality for the stomach's owner to digest.

In fact, when it came down to the bare bones of Patch's downfall and his trip to the 'doghouse', it was sausages that were to blame.

He recalled that he was in the kitchen that afternoon after returning home with Young Master, who had just finished his shift. While Tommy washed himself off of all the coal dust with water he had obtained from the outside pump and poured into the portable tin bath, Patch had decided to watch Mistress Ma making her pastries and was ready to help her tidy up any spilt food on the floor – a task which required infinite patience but it was an important one and he knew he was the perfect dog for the job. Patch had put his 'hunger' face on for good measure.

'Tommy, be a pet love, and go down to the butchers and ask Mr Fishwick for two dozen beef sausages, half a pound of skirt and any scraps. Make sure it's his best sausages and not his cheap ones, you can tell the difference. Oh, and see if you can get a beef bone for Patch; not a lamb bone mind you, it will splinter and catch in his throat.'

'Aye, Ma, I will,' replied Tommy. 'I'll take Patch. It'll keep him from staring at yer and the kitchen table all afternoon waiting for the next scrap.'

Ma smiled.

'Good idea, Tommy,' she said, 'but you better put him on a leash. Yer know what Patch is like when he gets near the butchers.'

Her son nodded. It was a rare occasion when he had to put his dog on a leash but a visit to Mr Fishwick's was definitely one of those when a restraint was a must. 'It fact a muzzle would not have been out of place,' grinned Tommy to himself.

Patch, naturally, didn't much take to having a rope tied around his throat and normally would have struggled with the same vehemence as he would if he had cornered a rat behind the screen sheds. However, when he heard the words 'butchers' and 'sausages' Patch went to 'hyperdoggy alert'.

The thought of him being in the sight and smell of sausages had sharpened all his senses; his taste buds began to stimulate his 'special sausage saliva'. The very word united all his doggy senses and he was sure that he could hear the distant cry of Mr Fishwick's sausages hanging off the metal hooks calling to him – 'Eat me!'

In a flash Patch was sitting obediently in front of Tommy – much to the latter's surprise – as still as a statue with his head bowed slightly forward, ready to allow his Young Master to slip the leash over his ears and attach it to his collar.

Patch strained every sinew and almost pulled his Young Master in the direction of the meat shop, and within a minute boy and dog were outside the village butchers.

'Now Patch,' said Tommy out loud as he tied the leash to a convenient iron post used to tether horses which was opposite the entrance to Mr Fishwick's, 'you stay here boy quietly, while I go in the shop. I won't be a few minutes.'

The little dog whined in frustration as his Young Master walked through the butcher's door. The whine was designed to illicit sympathy from the stoniest of hearts but Tommy ignored it, recognising the little dog's ploy, and shut the door to doubly make sure his pet could not enter.

'So near, so far from Doggy heaven,' lamented Patch to

himself. The dog lunged towards the door after his Young Master but any attempts to follow him just resulted in a painful yank on his neck.

It was torture to Patch seeing Young Master through the door talking to Mr Fishwick, who was serving behind the counter. He could also observe the lip smacking display of meats on the counter's metal trays, a side of beef carcass hanging from a ceiling hook, and next to it, more importantly to Patch, a string of succulent sausages.

Patch smacked his lips, more in anticipation than expectation.

Worst of all for Patch was that his nose was twitching in overdrive as the scent of the raw meat clung in the air and once in his nostrils only served to stimulate his over active taste buds.

'Now Bedlingtons are renowned for their discipline,' thought the little terrier, 'but even Bedlingtons have their limits. It's almost too much to bare!'

'Hello, Tommy lad,' greeted Mr Fishwick with a warm smile. ''Ope yer Ma is in good 'ealth. No reason not to be with the fine meats she eats from our shop, is there son?' Mr Fishwick laughed at his own remark.

With this the butcher began to rhythmically and noisily clash his meat knife on a sharpener, in theatrical fashion, no doubt with the intention of impressing both Tommy and his other customers in the shop – Mrs Popplethwaite and Mrs Maple, a tall, gangly widow ten years her junior but looking the same age.

Tommy turned and nodded politely to Mrs Maple and also Mrs Popplethwaite, who had wrapped around her left arm a basket full of groceries that she had bought that morning.

The two ladies smiled at 'the Wagstaff boy' and were content to allow him to be served before them as their visit to the butchers was not just for the purchasing of food for their tea that night but also as a place to hear and exchange the latest village gossip, of which Mr Fishwick was also a keen purveyor.

Tommy was a little wary when he saw Mrs Popplethwaite, who liked nothing better than relaying her tales of other villagers' business to anyone who would listen, especially if they were of someone else's misfortune, or better still, scandal.

'Where's your Ma?' probed Mrs Popplethwaite. 'Couldn't she make it today, lad. Hasn't had a funny turn again like, has she?'

Then she looked to Mrs Maple and added: 'Wouldn't surprise me – you do when you get to a certain age. I know I did.'

Mrs Maple nodded in sisterly agreement.

Tommy didn't like the way the conversation was going but refrained from taking her bait.

'She's fine, Mrs Popplethwaite. Thanks for askin',' replied Tommy, anxious to make his purchase and leave before any more interrogation.

'And where's your Patch, young Tommy? You never usually go around the village without your dog, lad,' probed the interrogator.

It was a good job too, thought Tommy, as Patch had taken an unusual instant dislike to Mrs Popplethwaite, even as a puppy when he would back away if she tried to stroke him. He knew Patch particularly did not like her cat, Genghis, a vicious, snarling, little brute who would claw and hiss at any passing object, man or beast.

'Just like its owner,' thought Tommy.

'Oh, 'e's outside, tied to the post, Mrs Popplethwaite,' he answered politely. 'I couldn't bring 'im 'ere, 'e'll be too excited,' replied Tommy, who quickly turned away from the ladies and pretended to take an interest in some lamb cutlets to avoid further conversation.

Tommy could see the relief on Mr Fishwick's face that his Patch was not in his shop.

'What d'yer want lad?' asked the butcher, having paused for breath after his 'sword display'.

'Ma wants her usual piece of skirt, please Mr Fishwick. A pound of scraps and two dozen beef sausages. Oh, and a beef bone for little Patch if yer 'ave one.

'Reet lad. Will do,' replied the butcher and set about the order.

'Eh, you're a credit to your Ma, Tommy Wagstaff,' complimented Mrs Popplethwaite, although not without a little sarcasm in her voice.

'So-oh respectful to your elders, and its lovely to see you and your Patch running wild through the village, even though the animal is off its leash and out of control.'

Tommy was indeed a polite lad and, perhaps, a little shy, especially in the company of his 'elders and superiors' but even he could not resist in responding to such barbed comments.

'If yer look out of the door you will see my Patch is safely tied to a post outside, behaving perfectly. Not that 'e needs a leash. Anyway, Mrs Popplethwaite, 'ow's yer cat Genghis getting on? I heard he went for Mr Fishwick's delivery boy Cyril last week when 'e was on his bicycle. Isn't that reet, Mr Fishwick?'

Mr Fishwick quickly turned his attention to finding a beef bone to avoid getting involved in any other customer confrontation.

However, Mrs Popplethwaite's face began to flush at the 'indignation'.

'That wasn't my Genghis' fault. That stupid Cyril nearly ran over his tail. And it's not my fault if young Cyril can't steer properly,' a clearly flustered Prudence Popplethwaite spat out in defence of her beloved moggy.

'I doubt if the cat's bite marks in his buttocks helped Cyril's steering either,' offered Tommy, ''Ow is Cyril by the way, Mr Fishwick?'

'Really!' exclaimed a clearly annoyed Mrs Popplethwaite, 'How dare you take that attitude with me, Tommy Wagstaff.'

The tension in the shop was beginning to rise like one of Ma's Yorkshire puddings in her oven.

'My Genghis is a real pussy cat compared with your Patch,' shouted an irate Mrs Popplethwaite. 'Your brute of a dog has caused more trouble in this village than any other animal I know. Just ask Mrs Curtois-Pughs; he's always frightening her poor little Archie, who's such a sweet little thing.'

Tommy was brought up to be respectful to his elders but this latest accusation was just too much.

He snapped back at Mrs Popplethwaite in his dog's defence, angered that she had portrayed his Patch to be unruly and vicious while her precious Genghis and the dreadful little yapper Archie were painted as models of good behaviour.

Tommy looked the woman straight in the eye before exclaiming in a loud, clear voice for the benefit of not just Mrs Popplethwaite but also Mr Fishwick and Mrs Maple.

'With all due respect, Mrs Popplethwaite, Our Patch is a loyal, affectionate little dog who has never bitten anybody in his life,' he exclaimed. 'Not like your Genghis. And I tell yer another thing, misses. Yer will never find a better behaved dog in the whole of the North Riding, let alone Hillthorpe!'

It was at that very moment that Tommy's world seemed to turn to a dream-like state and everything to him appeared to go in to slow-motion, although in reality the proceedings were over in a flash. For coming towards him at a rate of knots from the butcher's back room was Patch, freed from his leash, heading toward Mr Fishwick who was just about to reach up to unhook the beef sausages.

The timing was perfection. Patch bounded out of the back room of the shop and focussed on his target. The little terrier was in his 'hunter mode', which combined with his ravenous nature, at that moment took precedence over all other of his canine instincts.

In one flowing, sublime moment of magnificent movement Patch jumped onto the butcher's table next to the counter and from there sprang onto the counter itself; he then leapt with all his might and with balletic grace at a spot between the shoulder blades of Mr Fishwick, who, at that instant, had his hands stretched out above his head to remove his best sausages from the hook. With his front paws using Mr Fishwick as further leverage, Patch then launched his body by corkscrewing himself, above the butcher's head, to reach out and grab the sausages between his teeth. It was aerial ballet of the highest form. After gripping Mr Fishwick's finest between his jaws Patch pirouetted to the ground and tumbled – on what he termed when later reflecting on the moment from the comfort of his own blanket – into his 'sausage roll'.

The outstretched Mr Fishwick did not stand a chance; the unexpected shove in the back by the little dog caused him to lose balance and he staggered forward right onto the, equally unfortunate, Mrs Popplethwaite.

It was a sight young Tommy would remember for the rest of his life, as would the other entertained observer in the form of Mrs Maple. They witnessed Mrs Popplethwaite with the wind completely knocked out of her bellows, gasping for air with her legs inelegantly, fully stretched out in opposite directions in the air, with the not inconsiderable bulk of Mr Fishwick on top of her.

'That's the first time I've seen Mrs Popplethwaite speechless!' thought Tommy.

It was not a good time for Mr Fishwick either as, per chance, at that very moment in came the not inconsiderable bulk of Mrs Fishwick, who, after a visit to the village baker, had just arrived through the shop's front door. At the sight that confronted her she let out a disturbing, penetrating scream, one that even bruised the sensitivity of Patch's ears. There, before Mrs Fishwick's eyes, was her husband in an uncompromising position on top of the village gossip, while other customers looked on.

With the contents of Mrs Popplethwaite's morning shopping strewn all over the floor, never was a more chaotic scene seen in the local butchery.

As for Patch, with his prey still clenched between his teeth, he came out of his 'sausage roll' and took the opportunity to make his convenient escape through the front door thanks to the timely entrance of Mrs Fishwick – and before anybody

'That's the first time I've seen Mrs Popplethwaite speechless!' thought Tommy.

could utter the word 'sausages' he was out into the refuge of the street followed by a string of dangling beef bangers.

Tommy was absolutely gobsmacked at the events he had just witnessed but had the presence of mind to realise his presence was not probably a good idea once Mr Fishwick and Mrs Popplethwaite had regained their composure, if not their dignity. So he slammed down the money Ma had given him on top of the counter and – deciding to come back later for his order – with the relief of an excuse to flee the scene, gave chase after his mischievous mutt.

Once outside the door he looked in disbelief at seeing the abandoned leash still tied to the iron post. Tommy scratched his head.

'Ee Our Patch, thee must be some sort of Houdini hound to get out of that un,' he said to himself before he resumed his pursuit of his canine friend.

The events of that afternoon in the village butcher's shop soon rebounded on the little terrier. The irate figures of Mr Fishwick and Mrs Popplethwaite, accompanied by Mrs Maple – the latter who went along for the promise of further entertainment – were soon furiously knocking on the door of the Wagstaff household.

Ma, warned by her son of Patch's misdemeanour, which was confirmed when they both opened the back door and found their family pet stretched out in the sun, a picture of contentment, as he consumed yet another sausage in front of Da's pigeon coop.

Ma, in response to the continuous loud rapping on the front door, reluctantly opened it only to be immediately met by a volley of verbal abuse from the posse of Mrs Popplethwaite and a cross, but slightly embarrassed Mr Fishwick. Ma apologised to the assembled on her doorstep for her dog's actions, which she said were 'totally unlike Patch's normal level of behaviour,' to which Mrs Popplethwaite replied with a large grunt.

'Hmmm,' she snorted with her arms folded and implying it was certainly not the first time that Patch had misbehaved in such a manner.

'Of course, Mr Fishwick,' added Ma sounding as sweet as she could and looking directly at the butcher, 'I am sure if the contents of your sausages were not of such a high quality then Patch would never have been tempted to take such extreme actions.'

While this brought about a beam to the face of Mr Fishwick it just brought about another, but louder, 'Hmmm' from Mrs Popplethwaite, who refolded her arms yet again to emphasis her displeasure.

The matter was brought to a conclusion when Ma, dipping into the tin on the kitchen shelf, where she kept her scant savings for such 'emergencies', found a few shillings and pence to pay off Mr Fishwick for the loss of his sausages; this included also paying twice the amount again to 'satisfy' Mrs Popplethwaite to over compensate for her 'lost' vegetables.

Ma was not a happy woman – not just because of the pecuniary loss but at having to endure the humiliation and indignity of seeing that 'awful Mrs Popplethwaite' relishing every second of her embarrassment.

Patch was certainly in the doghouse!

That night in his bed the Bedlington reflected on his adventures that day and rued the fact that the sausages he had eaten earlier in the afternoon were now, unfortunately for his stomach, a distant, pleasurable memory.

'It's just not fair,' he reasoned to himself on his perceived punishment by Mistress Ma. It's just not fair!'

With that he slowly began to count, once again, the number of sausages on the string he had 'liberated' from Mr Fishwick's the butchers.

'Sausages,' was his last image before sleep eventually caught up with the little terrier, who once more was a picture of contentment as he snored and snoozed, lying on his beloved blanket.

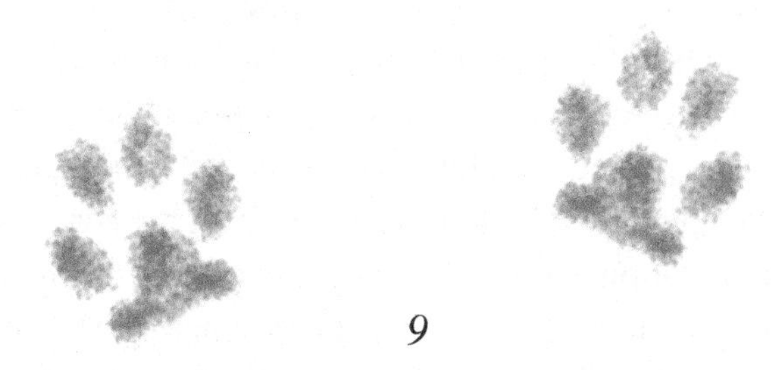

9

Bedlington's Never Back Down

IT was a dark winter's night in the North Yorkshire pit village; a cold snap lingered in the northern air and the stars twinkled, standing out in the black sky like the lit embers blazing amongst the coals of Da's fire.

During the day all the dogs of the village – except Archie, of course, who was far above such 'common canine collaborations' as he put it – decided to meet for a 'bow-wow' at the Colliers' Arms. Some of them even decided to take their masters and towed them along on their leads. There was no particular 'bone of discussion' on the agenda, just a pack get together in the comfort of the pub snug; it just happened to have a welcoming and well stoked fire attended by Arthur Tankard, the pub's landlord.

Mr Tankard was the owner of a pot-belly and ruddy complexion, typical of many a man in his profession. Thankfully he was not adverse to having dogs in his establishment, being a pet owner himself. In fact, his whippet, Slipper, was the fastest dog in the village – and duly named because he could never wait to be left off the leash, especially when it came to the whippet or course races at the annual district Miners' Gala. Slipper was 'as fast as lightning'. Unfortunately for Mr Tankard, who liked the odd flutter – or two (or three) – the energetic dog could never win its owner any prize or betting money because, although he was 'first out of the blocks' and always led from the start, Slipper had the orientation skills of a Friday night drunk trying to find his home from the Colliers' Arms after a skin full. The amiable whippet reared off in all directions – all except the finishing line. It also did not help that he was slightly cross-eyed.

It was not often Da went for a drink, not like most of the miners in the village, and Ma would certainly not begrudge her man the 'odd pint or two' even though money was tight.

'Go on Da, you enjoy yerself pet. Yer deserve it with the shifts yer put in this week. Besides,' said Ma, 'it'll do yer good to lubricate yer throat a bit and damp down the coal dust on your chest.'

Da, whether to emphasise the point or possibly just by chance, began to cough loudly but wasn't the sort of man to look a gift horse in the mouth.

'Aye, I think I will luv,' he replied when he regained his breathe from his coughing bout. 'Perhaps Patch could do with a stroll.'

By the time Da turned around to get his cap and jacket off the door peg, Patch was already sitting eagerly at the door with the leash firmly clenched between his teeth – a look on his face as if to say: 'Come on Master, what took you so long?'

All the Wagstaffs laughed at the sight, for they knew Patch had been waiting in that position for a full five minutes, even before Ma had suggested to Da that he should 'treat himself down the Colliers.'

As soon as Da and Patch arrived, his Master made for a

seat at one end of the grate by the fire, eager to find a warm place as the chill made him 'chesty' and induced his coughing fits.

Patch obediently sat down quietly at the feet of his Master and looked around him to take in the scene of miners, some of their wives and their dogs. Slipper came over and Patch wagged his tail in friendly acknowledgement before the pub dog disappeared behind the bar in search of a snack.

On the opposite side of the fire there was Gorse, a handsome ('well nearly as handsome as me,' thought Patch), black Labrador, who was more than a regular visitor to the village watering hole; the good natured dog had brought along his owners, Peter and Mary Tavy.

'I've nothin' against that dog, who like me loves lying by my fire. But Gorse, what a stupid name for a dog,' pondered Patch.

'Why would anyone call a dog that?' he asked himself.

After some considerable deliberation Patch concluded: 'Well, I suppose Gorse sounds as if he runs wild on the moors. . .

'Just like me. . .

'And is considered untameable and prickly. . .

'Just like me. . .

'And is full of tics. . . '

Patch let this final thought hang in the air, as he tilted his head after becoming suddenly distracted and feeling the urge to raise a right hind paw using his claws to scratch just behind his right fore ear, in search of what turned out to be an imaginary flea!

He was half way through satisfying this itch when his roving eye caught hold of another cute looking Labrador a few feet away, this time of the opposite sex. Now Patch, when it came to the ladies, prided himself in being 'a bit of a dog'.

After the recent disappointment of what he thought was finding his 'true love' with that mysterious, wondrous vision he had seen but not heard (or indeed smelt) outside Hardwick's ironmongery, Patch was looking for a little 'doggy' romance, and Jess, a beautiful, young Labrador was a right up his ginnel.

Of course, Patch was never put off by the fact that Jess was more than twice his size. Besides, he liked a bit of a challenge.

'Slick coat, shiny nose and a classy chassis. What's not to like?' he drooled.

With Da engrossed in a game of dominoes alongside his fellow miner and pigeon fancier, Cyril Pilcher, and his leash loose and out of his master's hand, Patch made his move on the delightful Jess.

He sauntered over in confident, if not cocky, style and decided, in true doggy fashion, to greet his intended paramour by sniffing the glands of her rear end; Jess, who suddenly felt a cold, wet nose thrust into her sensitive region, turned around in a spin, surprised at the little terrier's advances, and gave a high pitched, feminine yelp at the unexpected attention.

Patch was in mid-thought, thinking, 'My Dog, she don't half smell a bit of all right,' when all of a sudden he felt a gust of bad breath and the unnerving sight of a set of great big slobbering jaws right in his snout. This was followed by a loud, aggressive bark that caused Patch's ears and fur to fly backwards in the opposite direction to where he was looking, such was its intensity.

The big bark came from Mollie, a normally friendly, docile, if not rather somewhat lazy, Alsatian cross, who was Jess's best dog mate and self-appointed protector. She was usually just content to lay down next to the more lively Jess and keep an eye on her ward but she took her duty of chaperone seriously; when she spotted the brazen Bedlington stick his nose where it wasn't wanted, it stirred the sleeping giant.

So taken back with this thunderous 'woof' from Mollie – and even he admitted later to himself, it was nearly as loud as his famous 'Bedlington Roar' – that Patch put all four of his paws into quick reverse gear at such a speed that he knocked into the table Da and Mr Pilcher were sitting at, causing not only all their dominoes to go flying but also spilling Da's precious stout.

Da was not amused, and after only recently getting over his infamy over the sausage saga at the village butchers – following which he was in the doghouse with Ma – Patch now found himself occupying the same kennel, metaphorically, with Da.

Matters were made even worse by all the pub regulars, the landlord and most of all the other dogs, and Tipples, the pub cat, all laughing at his amorous attempts.

'It's just not fair,' thought Patch, as he now found himself pulled away by Da, well from reach of his intended sweetheart. With his back against the wall now, all he could see was the table and Da's legs.

'That Jess is a real flirt,' he grumbled to himself. 'I don't know about Jess, Jezebel more like. She fancies me rotten, I can just tell.'

Having regained his senses from the frontal assault by

Mollie, Patch responded vocally with a vengeance, his machine-gun like bark aimed directly at the over protective Alsatian.

Patch was absolutely seething at the humiliation, especially in front of all the other dogs and the cat. It was as if a red mist had descended upon him and there was one thing a Bedlington terrier never did when it came to a scrap – that was to back down to an opponent, no matter how big or ferocious they were.

'That dog is more cross than Alsatian,' reasoned Patch, who was now ready for the next round, which was rather timely as Mr Tankard rang the brass bell for 'last orders'.

Mollie was adamant and she too stood her ground, upholding her matronly honour as well as Jess's alleged virtue.

The Bedlington terrier and Alsatian squared up to each other, if square up was the phrase, as this mismatch in size was akin to Jack Johnson, the world boxing champion, going nose to nose with Charlie Chaplin. They both bared their teeth and snarled, with each antagonist prepared to fight to the kill.

Jess, feigning disinterest in the contest, coquettishly stood there with as much elegance and poise as she could muster, secretly content that she was the object of two dogs ready to fight 'for her honour' and looking forward to the bloody brawl.

But then, as the whole pub went silent at the anticipation of the 'prize fight', a very strange thing happened. Da realised his brave little belligerent Bedlington was set to spring into battle and knew that once the pugnacious breed drew blood that his Patch would not yield until 'victory or death'. So, just in the nick of time, he grabbed Patch by the collar, bent down beside his pet dog, cupped his hand and whispered something in the terrier's ear.

Immediately the dog turned with a puzzled but excited, if not soppy, look on his face and gazed at his Master. In an instant he completely calmed down and it was as if he was a different animal – calm and gentle with, if it was possible, a dreamy doggy smile on his face.

Mollie, normally a gentle soul herself unless ruffled or having Jess's honour to protect, wagged her tail, happy to let 'by dogs be by dogs' and was content to resume her place lying down next to her Labrador friend now the danger was averted.

'By 'eck Joe', a bemused Cyril Pilcher asked Da. 'Whatever did yer say to Patch to calm him down so quickly, like? I've never seen anythin' like it.'

Da once again cupped his hand and leant over to his friend and whispered in his ear – soft enough so Patch could not hear the golden words repeated.

Da revealed his secret calming words: 'Sausages, Cyril. Sausages.'

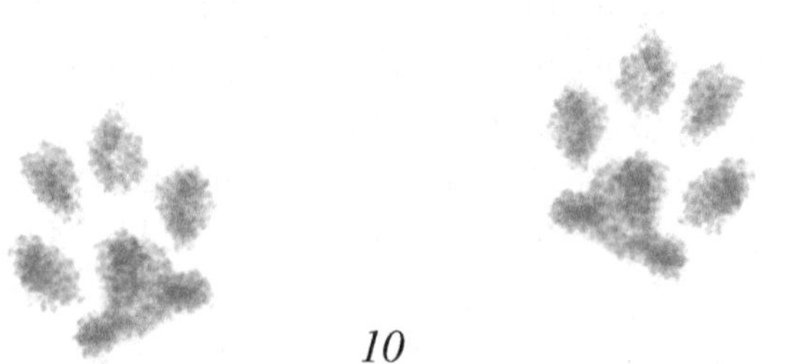

10

Gloom 'n' Groom

A HIGHLIGHT of the Wagstaffs' calendar, which coincided with one of Patch's 'pet hates', was his twice a year 'scrub' – normally performed by Mistress Ma and Young Master in early spring and late summer.

The ritual affronted every doggy instinct that the little terrier possessed. He could sense that his time was up for his 'impending doom' when Mistress Ma asked Young Master to carry the tin tub out onto the outside cobbles, while she took out her oldest, torn up cloths and blanket from her wooden chest. In Patch's mind it was the most barbarous torture known to a Bedlington but, with the doors to the cottage firmly shut and Young Master suddenly pouncing on him from behind, there was no escape.

What made it worse for Patch was that his 'torture' was actually condoned by fellow pack members – as Edward, Victor, and even the lovely Emma herself joined his 'torturers' – Mistress Ma and Young Master – in this 'spectator sport'.

No, a distraught Patch thought, it was a betrayal by those he loved and obeyed. He wriggled and barked and fought with all his might to escape Young Master's clutches but to no avail, as the larger pack member successfully clung on to the squirming dog with equal tenacity. Of course, he could have bitten his way out if he really wanted to by clamping his jaws around Young Master's hand to escape in the most extreme circumstances; however, the loyal Patch would not 'bite the hand that fed him' and considered such an action 'hitting below the collar'.

With Victor holding the front door ajar to facilitate dragging his 'victim' to the torture chamber of the front doorstep, and Edward fetching water from the village pump, Patch's fate was sealed.

Now clamped between Young Master's legs there was no escape as Edward handed Victor the first jug.

Patch, whose eyes belied the terror he knew was about to befall him, made one last effort to wriggle free; he stared up to Mistress Ma, pleading with her for mercy, and when she ignored him he turned his gaze to the more susceptible Emma, but again, to no avail. Even his highest pitch whine, with a double dose of whimpering and trembling, could not save him from the dreaded drenching.

It was as if young Victor took a special glee in it, thought Patch, as the boy raised the jug above his head and 'baptised' him with the full force of the torrent of water. As the cold, liquid poured down over his forehead, his ears and nose before it headed south toward invading the rest of his body, Patch suddenly froze to the spot; every sinew and muscle, every fur tip, stiffened in shock.

This was all too much for Patch, who then let out the loudest 'Bedlington Roar' he could muster, by whatever scale it could be measured on, and his machine-gun bark

One of Patch's 'pet hates', was his twice a year 'scrub'!

resonated off the cobbled road, bounced off the stone walls of the close-knit cottages to carry its deafening effect to the other houses down the rest of the little street.

Four houses down the road, in the lounge of collier Horace Cartwright and his wife, they sat at the table eating their dinner.

The latter said: 'Aweh, Horace, sounds as it must be wash day for Our Patch.'

'Aye luv,' came the reply, before continuing to cut up his boiled potato.

The 'torture' was not over for 'Our Patch'. As soon as the water took its icy hold, the next stage of assault began with Ma and Emma moving in with scrubbing brush and carbolic soap. Patch could feel a squadron of fleas on his body crawling for cover simultaneously, like rats abandoning a sinking ship.

With all the water and soap it was not long before Tommy's vice-like grip with his hands began to slacken; it was the chance the young dog had been waiting for and he wriggled free to liberty, but not before Victor had managed to drown Patch with a second large jug of water.

Torn away from his shackles Patch was now able to perform his bi-annual 'doggy hyper dryer' where, with four paws firmly rooted on the ground, head down, he went into 'super spin', shaking his torso so hard that droplets of water sprayed any unfortunate within a range of three yards of the little terrier. It was certainly unfortunate for Victor, who got a real soaking, being closest. Mind you, it was Victor whom Patch had chosen for this particular 'honour' after he observed how much delight 'the young pup' had pouring the jugs of water over him in the first place!

It was then, when Patch had just completed his 'doggy hyper dryer' that Ma and Tommy dived in – as they knew, through previous experience, that this was their only chance to pounce before their pet regained his wits and had time to bolt down the road to make his escape. While Tommy, once more, grabbed hold of Patch with an iron grip, Ma flung herself at the terrier and covered him with a raggedy old blanket and began to rub firmly the flanks of the freshly cleansed canine.

Patch grumbled and growled – well more grumble than growl – because by this time he began to admit to himself he did feel much cleaner and loved it when Mistress Ma gave him a good rub down. Having the undivided attention of most of the Wagstaff pack – Master Da was at work down the mine – was also a treat but that didn't stop Patch make the odd whimper to pretend his dissatisfaction.

No, what really got to the young Bedlington was when Emma decided to take over proceedings from Mistress Ma and Young Master.

Oh yes, he loved the tickling of his tummy and being rubbed and patted with a cloth by the lovely Emma, but then she pulled out another instrument of torture – a doggy comb.

She used the comb to pick and tease at Patch's coat until his fur, or fleece, was coaxed to its finest.

Being a Bedlington, he now took the appearance of a miniature sheep and it was made worse by all the rest of the Wagstaff pack looking at him with big grins on their snouts.

After Young Mistress Emma had done her best – although to Patch it was more like 'her worst' – the little dog's 'torture' finally came to an end as he slipped away from her loving clutches.

His anguish did not quite end there, as passing by, leaving their owners indoors, were Slipper and Gorse, out for a stroll. They could not but be shocked by Patch's new bouffant hairstyle and this was not helped when Slipper barked at him.

Patch slightly misheard, due to still having some soap in his ears. When Slipper, from across the road, woofed in doggie language 'Bad luck, lad' in sympathy with his pal's plight, Patch interpreted it as a long 'Baaa' and took umbrage. In 'two shakes of a lamb's tail' this sent Patch into a foul mood. With that the little terrier headed for the nearest grassy spot and rolled on his back, kicking his legs into the air like a disgruntled mule; soon his freshly washed fleece took a more natural form.

When he returned to the house, Mistress Ma was not pleased.

That night Patch was, once more, in 'the dog house'.

11

Never Trust a Cat

'CATS,' Patch concluded, 'were useless animals, no use to dog or beast.' Indeed, he could not see their purpose or why the 'Great Bedlington in the Sky' had created such a creature, except, of course, as some sort of curse to the canine species – as to why dogs had to be punished in such a way by the Great Master was beyond the little terrier.

'Dogs were noble, obedient, useful creatures, loyal,' he mused, 'dependable, affectionate and friendly – well all except for that lah-di-dah Archie – but cats!' Patch snorted. . . 'They are just vicious, self-seeking, manipulative animals – not like us dogs. They jump up on places where they don't belong; lay stretched out in the sun with nothing to do; pull down the clothes off Mistress Ma's washing line with their claws and drop dead mice on the kennel doorstep.

'Yuk!' Patch visibly shuddered at the thought. 'And fur balls, what's that about? I've never seen a cat choke on one, more's the pity.'

'. . .and, Oh My Dog, don't they smell terrible!' he added as an afterthought.

Patch became more and more agitated as he pondered in greater depth on the baffling subject of the feline species.

'They are so sly,' Patch continued. 'One minute a cat will scratch or bite its own mistress and the next moment she will forgive it just because it rubs itself against her legs and purrs. She will even pick it up and stroke the mangy moggy. If I bit Mistress Ma I'd be in the dog house for a week, or she could even order me to pack my collar and find a new kennel to live in!

The rant continued. . .

'How Slipper manages to live in the same room as that pub cat Tipples, I do not know! She even has the cheek to steal his place by the fire in the evening and he doesn't even lift a paw.'

'Mind you,' Patch recalled with satisfaction 'Tipples can't get away fast enough when I walk in with Master through the door. She knows not to mess with a Bedlington!'

The prickly subject of 'cats' had come to Patch's mind because of three members of the species in particular.

Five doors down, on the opposite side of the terrace of miners' cottages, lived two of these felines – Flossie and Socks. They belonged to their mistress, Mrs Stefferson, whose husband was a carpenter at the mine; their family was completed by their two children, Freda and Maxwell. In fact, it was the persistence of the children, and Freda in particular, who every birthday and Christmas 'begged and pleaded and begged again' for a kitten, that eventually led to their parents relenting; and so, to be fair to both children, they decided to 'adopt' two kittens to avoid further 'cat fights' among their bairns.

The two bundles of fur were as different as two cats could

be and definitely not from the same litter. Socks, a black tom cat with white flashing, was athletic and nimble; akin to many of its species it had a degree of curiosity which, not unlike Patch himself, often more times than not, resulted in getting him into a spot of trouble. If there was a tree to climb, a hole to explore, a mouse to chase, Socks was the cat for the job.

Flossie, although the same age, was certainly not a ball of energy compared to her more vibrant 'brother' but tended, as befitted her tubby frame, to be more sedate, even lazy. She had 'tiger' like stripes of grey and fawn, an unusual though distinctive colouring, but 'tiger' she was not. For Flossie loved nothing better than doing nothing all day but lie in the sun (Northern climate permitting), or, better still, to feel the warmth of the fire on her fur as she stretched out in front of the hearth. Flossie was an affectionate, mild mannered cat who just let the world go by. If one of the children picked her up for a cuddle she would purr with delight. Her sedentary nature did not apply, of course, when it came to meal times, as despite her rotund figure, somehow she always managed to beat Socks to the latest feed put down by her mistress – much to the annoyance of the aggressive tom, who spitefully used to barge Flossie out of the way, or give her a 'whack' with his paw but not, annoyingly for him, before the female had already enjoyed the first 'gulp'.

When it came to cats, Patch generally ignored them – 'cats should be not seen and not heard' was the terrier's philosophy. With Flossie, however, Patch did not have too much trouble – she did not even flicker a tail when he came near, never hissed at him, and was even known to meow a greeting to him now and again. More importantly Flossie knew 'the rules' – 'don't mess with dogs and dogs won't mess with you' and as long as she knew her 'place' Patch would tolerate her existence – not that he would admit it but he even developed a bit of a soft spot for the affable, cuddly cat.

As for Socks, well, he was a different kettle of fish. In fact, come to think of it, thought Patch: 'It was fish that had got Socks into serious trouble with him in the first place.'

On Sunday afternoons, weather permitting, Da would head for a spot of fishing along the banks of the River Ned, which ran to the south of the village. Angling for Da, along with his wood whittling, was among his favourite pastimes – not that he had much time on his hands – although nothing, of course, could beat his beloved homing pigeons. After spending all his working life in the heat and dark of the bowels of the earth, Da liked nothing better than being out above ground as nature intended and getting some fresh air in his lungs.

Da was often joined by his eldest son, who grabbed any opportunity to spend precious time alone with his father – Edward and Victor thought fishing was 'boring', just waiting around doing nothing for hours on end, while Emma hated the thought of watching the killing of any live creature – although she was still partial to eating trout if cooked by Ma.

Da had crafted his own simple rod out of hickory and used twine for the line. His tackle itself was second, or even third hand, which he had traded with another collier for Homer, one of his pigeons. The bird certainly belied his name as, whenever it tried to return to its coop when released, it was always the last of the flock home by far – so Da thought the exchange was quite a bargain at the time.

It was Tommy's 'job' to carry the bait – fresh maggots and stale bread crumbs. Even the ravenous Patch, who had happily joined them for the trip, turned his nose up at such fayre.

For hours Da would be content to cast his line and fly into the waters and sit patiently for a bite. Tommy, just happy to be with his father, would sit next to him with his own rod and line, while Patch either ran up and down along the riverbank within sight of his masters or, mostly, lay down next to them on the grass for a well-deserved 'snooze'.

Occasionally Da was rewarded for his patience when the odd brown trout would come his way, and even on memorable but extremely rare occasions, a prized salmon; a rare treat that Da would make a show of, presenting it with great pride to Ma in front of the rest of the family.

However, it was Tommy that usually bettered his father when it came to catching fish, much to Da's continual bafflement. Each time they went angling he could not understand his son's greater success. While Tommy knew the answer, he did not have the heart to reveal his secret to Da. It was his father's bout of coughing when in possession of the rod, which gave any potential catch warning of his presence and they would swim away to live another day.

So far five fish were their combined catch, and the two anglers proudly displayed their trophies behind them, lined up out on the grassy bank, while they returned their attention for trophy number six.

Patch gazed at the five brown scaly creatures, decided they smelt revolting and were too disgusting to eat, so resumed his dozing duties, ready to 'spring into action' when either of his masters had a 'tickle' on the line and the fun began.

Tommy was the next to reel in a little trout, and as soon as it was on land Da unhooked it and put the wriggling, gasping fish out of its misery. In high spirits Da and Tommy turned to place it with their growing collection.

'I thought we caught five fish Da, before this un, but now there's only five there, including the new un,' exclaimed Tommy, scratching his head.

'Aye, lad,' said Da, equally baffled, 'I've caught two and you've caught four, Tommy – this last one is number six. I don't understand.'

Now Patch, beginning to come out of his afternoon nap, was already making his own calculations. Obviously, being a Bedlington, counting was a handy skill, especially if you were looking at a string of sausages hanging up in the butchers. He, too, noticed that there were now only five fish lying there when there should have been six. This needed further investigation.

Reluctantly he got up to interrupt his 'doggy dreams', as he called them, went over to the five fish and began to sniff wildly. While his masters continued to deliberate the mystery of the missing trout Patch 'sprang' into action. After one part of his smelling senses came to terms with the stink of fish another part was already on the trail.

Following the scent, Patch scrambled up the riverbank and was in hot pursuit, closely followed by Tommy.

'What's up, Patch?' asked Tommy. 'Where are yer goin' boy?

But Patch had already solved the mystery.

'It could only be one thing,' thought Patch. 'And that thing is cat!'

His assumption was soon proved correct as just ten feet

away, under a bush, was one very contented little moggy chewing away on a tasty trout – Socks enjoying an unexpected afternoon snack.

The Bedlington Roar was the first warning that Socks had of the approaching Patch; he didn't wait around for a second, despite having to abandon half of the carcass which was already stripped down to the bone and decapitated – a state Patch intended to impose on the slippery Socks if he got his gnashers on him. The little black cat, having the presence of mind to keep some of his bounty between its jaws, made a smart get away and scampered up the nearest tree to escape by a whisker – just as Patch was about to pounce on the feline felon.

Patch barked up at Socks, who was now safely sat on a thick branch enjoying the rest of his fish dish – this really annoyed the terrier whose distinctive machine-gun like bark was now in overdrive, but despite his best effort its resonance could not shake the cat out of its hideaway.

'Come on, Patch. I don't think Socks will be coming down for a while. Besides, we've got the rest of the catch to get back to Ma for our tea.

'I think it's Socks 1 Patch 0,' said Tommy with a grin.

Patch was not a happy hound.

Tommy turned, picked up his gear and fishy treasure, and followed his Da down the riverbank path to head for home.

Patch looked up at Socks, who he swore had certainly turned into the Cheshire variety of its species, having a big wide grin on its face.

'I'll beat you, Socks. You just wait,' thought a clearly irritated Patch, who growled to himself before turning to follow his masters. 'Nobody beats a Bedlington, certainly not a pesky cat. This is not over, not for all the sausages in Fishwick's!'

Indeed it was not long before Patch returned 'the favour'. Two days later the terrier was quick to seize the opportunity presented to him by the 'Great Bedlington in the Sky' – for which he was truly thankful.

Socks and Flossie, on a hot summer's day, were outside their house enjoying the clement weather. While Flossie was lying down on the road, basking in the sunshine, Socks had strayed over to a nearby horse trough to go for a drink. With one athletic movement he leapt on to its stone edge, braking with its paws and finely balancing its body.

He bent down and pursed his mouth to lap up the cool, cold water for refreshment. Patch seized the moment. From across the street, and before Flossie had the time to miaow a greeting, the terrier ran at full pelt in advance of head-butting the unsuspecting tom cat straight into the trough.

'Socks 1 Patch 1,' thought Patch, who had the extra delight of hearing his adversary wailing in fright, with a sound that even made Flossie raise her head from her half slumber.

Patch jumped up so his paws were on the edge of the trough and he could see the panic in Socks's eyes as the cat flailed around desperately in the water with its paws, fighting for life and screaming with all its might in a sound that roused the whole neighbourhood.

Mrs Stefferson came running out of the house with little Freda and Maxwell scurrying behind her to see what all the commotion was about. They were just in time to witness an amazing sight that was often talked about in the Colliers' Arms for many years to come.

Patch, although still annoyed with Socks for stealing his masters' fish, leapt up on the trough's ledge and jumped into the water; this just added to the cat's distress, not that it needed any more at that particular moment. Then, incredibly, Patch opened his jaws wide and grabbed the cat by the scruff of the neck, holding its head up above the water to prevent it from going under. It was just long enough before a grateful Mrs Stefferson came to scoop the soaked Socks into her arms.

Patch scrambled out of the trough – it did not really matter that the water was only eighteen inches deep and he was actually standing on the base of the trough; he had done his job.

To the grateful Mrs Stefferson and her two even more grateful children, Patch was the 'hero of the hour' and soon he was the talk of the village.

'Go and get two blankets, Max,' ordered Mrs Stefferson before prudently adding, '. . .the old ones'.

Freda tried to calm down her beloved Socks, who was still recovering from his 'near death experience'.

'You still got eight lives to go,' Patch thought, with tongue firmly in snout.

Drenched through himself, the terrier decided it was time to go into 'doggy hyper dryer' but not before positioning himself right next to the unsuspecting Flossie who felt the full force of the little dog's shakings.

Soon Mrs Stefferson had her second oldest blanket around 'the hero', rubbing him till he was bone dry – 'Did someone mention bone?' queried Patch. The oldest and tattiest blanket was reserved for Socks.

'Yer won't be going that close to the water again, will yer

Socks?' admonished Mrs Stefferson. 'If it wasn't for Our Patch 'ere, you wouldn't be alive, yer silly cat.'

The 'modest' Patch then received a huge hug and a kiss from the lovely Freda, much to the consternation of the plainly jealous Socks, who once more screeched in indignation.

To make matters worse for Socks, and subsequently to the delight of Patch, the Steffersons rewarded the 'brave Bedlington' with three delicious sausages, freshly cooked.

Having finished his welcome snack, Patch made for home.

'Socks 1 Patch 2,' he concluded. 'You'll never beat a Bedlington.'

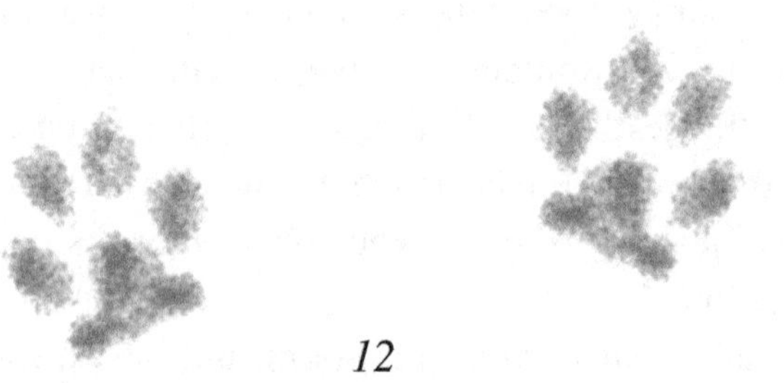

12

Genghis Can

IF there was one cat that Patch despised and hated above all it was Mrs Popplethwaite's half Mongolian cross, Genghis. What it was crossed with Patch could only wonder but it definitely, according to Hillthorpe's top dog, had never been baptised by the forces of 'Good'.

To Patch it was the perfect partnership of pet and owner and, of course, the village gossip lavished the same misguided affection and unearned ridiculous praise for her Genghis as did Mrs Curtois-Pughs with that excuse for a dog, Archie.

The sight or, indeed, the very name, of Patch's feline adversary was enough to send the shackles rising in his fur. To the terrier, Genghis represented all that was 'evil' in the species – a cat who was renowned and feared, in equal measure, among the animal population of Hillthorpe for its random viciousness and cruelty.

Many a time, behind the screens, Patch had witnessed Genghis toying with a terrified mouse – its paws standing firmly on its tail or its claws wrapped over its prey's trembling body. Genghis would delight in peering with its evil eyes close up to its prey, licking his lips in anticipation of the kill and bearing his ferocious fangs to intimidate the defenceless victim. Often the little rodent would give up its struggle after a good ten minutes of 'play' and drop down to the ground lifeless out of sheer exhaustion, and more often than not, sheer terror.

The fact also, observed Patch, that it was only mice, smaller rodents and fellow cats that Genghis targeted, confirmed to the terrier that Mrs Popplethwaite's puss was nothing better than a nasty, cowardly bully. Even the other cats in the village all detested the 'Mongolian monster' and there was not one dog either who had a good thing to woof about 'the Evil One'.

If ever Patch was passing on his 'rounds' and saw Genghis bullying some poor unfortunate then he felt it his duty to give his adversary 'a dose of its own medicine'.

Being of a cowardly nature and with a cunning instinct for self-preservation, Hillthorpe's most repulsive and despised creature always, somehow, managed to avoid Patch's lunging jaws and make its escape at the very last possible second; the wily Genghis would carry out a swift retreat by leaping to the nearest tree branch or ledge and, once safe from Patch's grasp, would look down at the frustrated terrier with a wicked sneer on its face and an expression as if to say 'You'll never catch me, you stupid dog.'

This just infuriated Patch even more and he vowed that one day he would have his vengeance on the malignant Mongolian moggy.

Of course, what Patch did not know was that in his coming to the rescue of many a mouse from the claws of 'the Evil One' the little dog was hailed as a bit of a hero among the

Hillthorpe rodent population. So much so, that the rats and mice collectively decided not to set up home anywhere within 25 feet of where their idol lived – which was quite an honour because they all knew that Ma Wagstaff, according to their annual 'rat ratings', was by far the best cook in the village bar none, although a few points were deducted because Mistress Ma was in the top five for domestic cleanliness, always sweeping her home and yard – not helped by the vigilant Patch himself, always on the lookout for discarded crumbs.

No, to the rodents, when it came to setting up a residence for a fast growing family, then 'Patch's pad' – as it was known by the local rats and mice – was considered a prime location. Thus, unbeknown to Patch, indirectly, he was helping to keep the Wagstaff 'kennel' squeaky clean of the local rodent population.

The rivalry between Patch and Genghis went back to the time they were puppy and kitten. Being of around the same age they had grown up together in the village.

The mutual dislike came from their first encounter – when their respective owners met one Tuesday morning at Fishwick's, both with their shopping baskets slung around their forearms. Patch was only a few months old and being a Bedlington, a typical of his breed, as a puppy he was just a slither of a thing. Both pup and kitten, being so small, were able to be tucked snugly and safely inside their owners' arm baskets, sharing space among the morning shopping.

That day was certainly a memorable one for Patch. Firstly, it was his first sight and smell of sausages, a delight that was to stay with him all his life. Secondly, it produced a memory that proved not quite so pleasant.

Mrs Popplethwaite was making her usual 'catty' remarks.

'Good morning, Mrs Wagstaff,' her opening salvo not an indication of the venom to come. 'I see your Tommy has a new puppy. I hope he looks after it. Young boys soon get bored with their pets, you know. It's not fair on the poor animal,' she opined.

'I see you have another kitten, Mrs Popplethwaite,' retorted an obviously annoyed but calm Ma. 'That must be your fourth in five years, isn't it? Yer seem to get through yer cats, Mrs Popplethwaite.'

This brought an instant reaction from the Hillthorpe tabby.

'You know full well two of those kittens had congenital conditions and everybody knows it was an unfortunate accident that my Siamese, Fang, fell down a well. Fortunately I have been blessed with a little darling of a kitten now, Genghis – a gentle, placid Mongolian – he's a rare pedigree, you know.'

To emphasise her point she raised her basket to show off her latest pet to Ma and the bemused Mr Fishwick.

'Say hello to Mrs Wagstaff and her little puppy, Genghis sweetie,' cooed the older woman.

Ma moved a little closer to appraise the object of Mrs Popplethwaite's admiration and the two baskets touched. Patch, rocked and woken by the movement, inquisitively came out to peer over to greet the feline bundle of fur and poked his head into Mrs Popplethwaite's basket. With that Genghis omitted a vicious hiss and proceeded to flick out a paw – smack on Patch's nose. Patch, only trying to be friendly and being totally unprepared for such an unsuspecting assault, gave his first official 'Bedlington Roar' – although what actually came out was more like a high pitched 'Bedlington Whelp'.

'Nasty brute,' exclaimed Ma, shocked by the viciousness of the unprovoked attack. 'It seems to 'ave a nasty nature, Mrs Popplethwaite,' before adding, 'I don't know where it picked that up from.'

'Nonsense,' an indignant Mrs Popplethwaite replied, 'how dare you accuse my defenceless little Genghis. He wouldn't harm a fly. Anybody could see your puppy started it. My kitten was just trying to protect itself. You saw that, didn't you, Mr Fishwick?'

'Oh. . . no. . . Mrs Popplethwaite. I wuz weighin' up yer scrag end at the time. I. . . I. . . I didn't see anything,' he stuttered, before pretending to turn his attention elsewhere.

'And I will thank you to keep your vicious mongrel away from my pedigree cat in future, Mrs Wagstaff.' Mrs Popplethwaite delivered her final broadside in a huff of indignation as the 'victim' in this affair.

An increasingly miffed Ma turned to go out of the door.

'Come on, Patch,' she replied sharply, 'I don't want you catching any fleas from that moggy. But I won't worry boy, that Genghis won't be around for long if her owner's past history of lookin' after cats is anything to go by.'

Mrs Popplethwaite's face turned from its usual reddish complexion to 'iridescent purple' and temporarily – very temporarily – she was lost for words; she peered into her basket to reassure her kitten and cooed: 'There, there Genghis. That nasty dog has gone now, my precious.'

With that she put her hand in the basket in order to stroke her kitten but the same hand was withdrawn at a rate of knots as its owner screamed in pain from a spiteful scratch bestowed by the claw of her 'little baby'.

In such a small village it was inevitable that the paths

of Patch and Genghis were destined to cross and cross they did.

Patch would never forget the time that the 'Mongolian menace' as the whole village called him – apart from his owner, of course – visited the very heart of the Wagstaff kennel. Neither would Ma!

A young Patch was having his well-deserved afternoon nap on his blanket after fulfilling his duties for that day; he was biding his time before his next job in around an hour – meeting the children from school and escorting them home. Mistress Ma was in the kitchen, rolling out pastry and sprinkling it with flour.

'Oh Patch,' she muttered, mainly to herself, 'I've run out of butter so I'd better go down t' the shop for 'alf a pound.'

Patch did not bat an eyelid. Normally he would have escorted Mistress Ma to the shops but after such a 'hard day' decided his blanket was presently too comfortable to leave – besides, he reasoned, he had to go to work soon.

Ma took the money from her tin on the Welsh dresser, wrapped herself in her shawl and took three steps to the door; she went to shut it behind her but, unbeknown to her, as she did so the latch bounced back, leaving the door slightly ajar. Patch was irritated by the slight draught but the bedded Bedlington could not be bothered to get up to shut it properly. It was a tactical mistake!

Patch briefly raised himself up to reposition himself and turned his body in the basket before flopping down a few seconds later to resume his snooze.

A few minutes after Ma's departure, Genghis made his move. The temptation of an open door was too much for the curious cat, even though he knew it would be intruding on 'enemy' territory. After carefully poking his head around the door and seeing Patch asleep, he slid in the rest of his stubby body and entered the kitchen/parlour.

Genghis smiled menacingly to himself, before peering around the room to fix his bearings. He glanced at the fireplace and, to the cat's delight, spotted a couple of ornaments conveniently decorating the mantelpiece. Genghis swiftly went into action, hoping to cause as much damage as possible in the shortest possible time, before heading for his planned 'escape route'.

He then jumped up to the mantelpiece, via a convenient coal scuttle, and deftly strolled across its length towards the intended target, before purposely giving it a 'nudge' with his paw; the delicate china object tumbled onto the stone of the hearth, smashing the ornament into pieces with a mighty crash. The din awoke the dozing Patch, who, once back from 'the land of dog', saw the shattered vase strewn all over the floor, before looking up at the perpetrator.

Genghis was not finished with his 'invasion' yet, determined to do more vandalism and create more havoc before leaving the scene of the crime. From the mantelpiece, in two leaps, and showing his agility which belied his stout, unathletic appearance, the cat pounced onto Da's chair, which he then used as a springboard before launching himself at the window curtains; when he dug his front paws into the material, there was no letting go until Genghis had ripped the curtain off its rail.

Patch, completely taken by surprise at the attack on his kennel, was now in a real rage at the bold affront by the despised Genghis. He flung himself, with all his might, at the cat when the tom fell to the floor.

Much to Patch's annoyance, the sly Genghis anticipated this move and in the blink of an eye made for the safety of the table. To make matters worse for Patch, his momentum from diving at, and missing, the intruder meant that he lost his 'paw grip' on Ma's freshly polished floor and went straight into the wall below the window.

Patch squealed, more with indignity and exasperation than physical pain; he turned to face his feline foe but Genghis just purred in delight at the dog's ineptitude and strolled arrogantly across the top of the table, before deliberately knocking over Ma's bag of flour which she had left open. Patch, putting his paws on a chair, used it to clamber up onto the table itself, but with his wide open jaws he was not fast enough to grab hold of the cat before it had made more of a mess with the remains of the flour.

For the next two minutes there was absolute pandemonium as Patch chased the feline felon in the downstairs confines of the little cottage; furniture was knocked over, Ma's knitting ball unravelled, plates were smashed and the coal scuttle tumbled over, scattering its dirty black contents all over the floor.

After having a quick glance at the resulting destruction due to his visit, Genghis, who was having the time of one of his nine lives, was more than satisfied with his four minutes 'work'. He then decided it was time to make his escape through the gap in the open front door – which the cunning cat knew was just ajar enough for him to squeeze through but not the more sizeable Patch.

To make matters worse for the terrier, just as he was trying to prize open the door with his front right paw so he could continue his chase of the elusive Genghis, suddenly appearing on the doorstep in front of Patch was Mistress Ma herself.

As she pushed the handle, Patch took the opportunity and bolted after the cat, bravely in pursuit of the intruder, ready to redeem the honour of the Wagstaff pack and administer justice to the vile perpetrator who had vandalised the family kennel. However, by now the crafty cat was nowhere to be seen, as Patch ran around in circles barking and growling and stamping his paws in rage.

But in the frenzy of the 'chase' Patch did not hear the scream of horror emanating from the lungs of his mistress after she was greeted, when arriving home, to a scene of utter devastation.

'PAAATCH!' roared Mistress Ma, as she came to the doorstep and summoned the 'family pet' – ex-family pet if her face was anything to go by.

'IN!' she commanded, and with arm outstretched Ma pointed her finger towards the front door and Patch instinctively knew that it was a command not to be questioned.

'I LEAVE YOU FOR FIVE MINUTES ALONE IN THIS HOUSE AND THIS IS HOW YOU BEHAVE!' she bellowed.

Patch visibly quivered at the sound of an enraged Mistress Ma, a voice he had never heard before.

'She's got a better Bedlington Roar than I've got,' he thought, almost with admiration but not without dreading what was to come. He whined and sank to the floor, his ears pinned back and giving the most pathetic look known to dog, but there was no stopping a livid Mistress Ma.

'Look at the mess you made. BAAAAD DOG. BAAAAD DOG!'

To make matters worse, when Patch and his mistress surveyed the apocalyptic scene together the latter accused him of being the sole perpetrator.

'Those are your paw prints all over the curtains and the floor you WICKED, WICKED DOG,' shouted Ma, who was almost losing her voice with rage.

'It was true,' thought Patch. 'All the paws prints are mine. You don't have to be Sherlock Bones to work that one out! But how can I tell Mistress that it was that mangy Genghis. That crafty moggy has made sure there is not one cat paw left at the scene of the crime. I've been framed!' concluded Patch and he barked with indignation.

'QUIET!' boomed Ma. Patch had never seen his beloved mistress so angry, so he decided to make a hasty, tactical retreat to his blanket.

'AND WHERE DO YER THINK YOU'RE GOIN'?' bellowed Ma. 'DON'T THINK YER GOIN' TO THE COMFORT OF YER BASKET AS IF NOWT HAS 'APPENED. . . YER BAAAAD, BAAAAD BOY!'

With that she picked up her sweeping brush and, before she started to tidy up, she took it to take a big swipe at Patch's rear end and began to 'brush' him towards the front door.

'OUT!' commanded Ma, again using her outstretched arm and pointing her finger towards the door, and it had not escaped the little dog that a heavy shower had begun to fall outside.

'What do you mean OUT, you just told me to get IN?' a bemused terrier queried of his mistress with beseeching eyes. There was no reply.

As Patch, with his tail between his legs, made his way into the street, his final humiliation was about to be fulfilled.

Then Mistress Ma said the words that Patch feared most and put a shiver down his spine.

'And there'll be no supper for you tonight boy. . .'

Patch put his downbeat face against the rain and shivered as the bite of a north westerly took its grip; the sad little terrier whimpered to himself at his misfortunate as his plea of innocence had fallen on deaf ears.

However, in true Bedlington style, Patch stubbornly refused to admit to himself he was beaten and was now even more determined to have his revenge on the 'Mongolian menace'.

As Patch sought shelter from the inclement elements he muttered and vowed to himself: 'I'm going to make that Genghis pay for this if it's the last thing I do. This is personal. This is war! I'll teach him to mess with a Bedlington.'

A riled Patch made his way to the Colliers' Arms to share his woe, and perhaps some shelter, some sympathy, and maybe a biscuit with his friend Slipper.

As he did so, across the street, looking down at him and perched high on the roof of the pigeon coop, was the 'Evil One' – purring with delight at the sorry sight of the despondent little dog dragging his way towards the village pub.

Between its teeth were the feathers of one of Da's former favourite pigeons, Homer. The bird, who had unfortunately decided to take refuge from the storm at his old home after losing his way when released by his new owner, could not get back into the coop before tragedy, or Genghis, had struck.

Although undoubtedly Patch, Mistress Ma and Homer would not agree, today, for Genghis, it had been a 'purrfect day'.

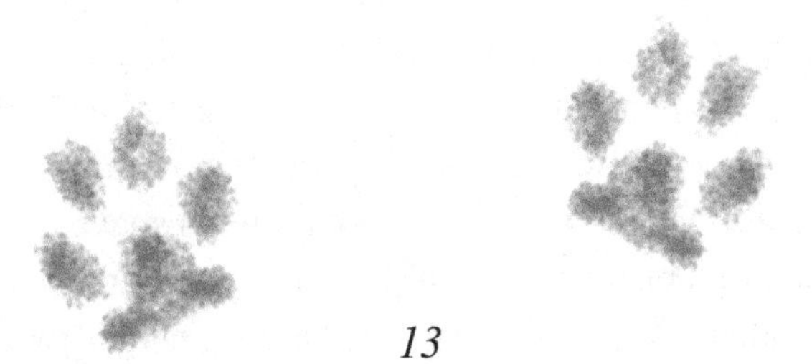

13

Quiet as a Church Mouse

UNLIKE the other members of the Wagstaff pack, there was one tradition that Patch was not required to join in with – attendance to Sunday services at Hillthorpe Methodist Chapel.

It was Ma, a spiritual soul herself, who felt it important, and to the benefit of her children, that they should be brought up in the Christian faith.

She had 'given up' on Da, who rarely attended. He preferred to spend his precious Sundays either caring for his pigeons or 'pottering around' in 'The Patch'. As a miner, Da had witnessed many a tragedy in his workplace which shook his belief in a caring and loving God. However, like many a collier, whether he admitted it or not, his nugget of faith in all that was good and just, had remained buried deep in his heart – down to an ember, maybe, but refusing to be extinguished forever and perhaps ready to glow again.

Very occasionally in the evening Ma would read out Bible stories to entertain the children and Patch would listen in. Although his mind was normally on his next meal, this particular evening he was concentrating and increasingly becoming annoyed on whether or not Young Master Edward was going to finish that biscuit he was nibbling!

'If he doesn't want to eat it, give it to me,' Patch pleaded silently to his fellow pack member, but to no avail as Edward continued to take his time in consuming his snack.

Although most of Mistress Ma's tales went 'in one ear and out the other' Patch's interest was held by one or two of the stories. His favourite was when a big brown trout swallowed whole this man called Jonah and then spat him out alive.

'I've never seen a fish that big in the River Ned. I thought all fish were tiny creatures – well, all the ones Young Master and Master Da catch always are,' he pondered.

Then there was a really disturbing story about this man called Daniel who was thrown into prison with four huge and ferocious cats and survived. Patch trembled at the prospect of being incarcerated with four giant Genghises.

'It would take four Genghises to get the better of a Bedlington,' Patch reassured himself, but that night he did not sleep well, tossing and turning in his basket during his 'doggy dreams'.

However, there was one chapel event that Patch always looked forward to and that was the annual 'Animal Service' conducted by Reverend Segdwick.

Hillthorpe Chapel was packed for the popular service, held on St Francis' day, the patron saint of animals – it was one of the highlights on the local church calendar.

Patch was in the back pews, along with his Mistress Ma, Young Masters Tommy, Victor and Edward and Young Mistress Emma. As a special treat on that day, pets were allowed to sit in the pews, if they wished, next to their owners.

Most of the village animals were there, certainly all the cats and dogs, along with a menagerie of creatures in the congregation. Cyril Pilcher had brought a basket of his homing pigeons; he hoped that if they were blessed they might have more chance of success in the forthcoming race in the Hillthorpe and Daleswick Miners' Gala.

A mile outside the village was Ramsdens' Farm, where Tommy and Patch often strolled past when they were 'on patrol'. Farmer Ramsden himself had brought along two of his piglets, which brought squeals of delight from the children present.

The 'star' attraction, although no doubt Patch, Genghis and Archie may have disputed this fact, was Dolly the donkey. Dolly was a well fed and mostly docile animal who belonged to Mr Bramley, the fruit and vegetable shop owner, who used her to pull a cart on his delivery round. Dolly made three annual appearances at the chapel – once at Christmas, when she played a leading role in the nativity play; another at Easter, when Dolly joined in the Palm Sunday procession where she always sported a straw bonnet, cut out to accommodate her big ears, and of course, the animal service itself.

Reverend Sedgwick was delighted with the turnout, both of people and their pets. Unknown to the minister the congregation was doubled in size by the local rodent population, who although unnoticed by the humans, were either below the floorboards or had taken their 'seats' behind the skirting boards.

The rats and mice were, unlike many of the humans in the village, regular attenders at Hillthorpe Methodist Chapel.

Patch sat quietly next to Tommy and on 'his Sunday best'

behaviour, looking around to see who else among his acquaintances were present.

There was the delightful Jess lying in the aisle he noticed; next to her was Jess's 'mistress' Molly with their owners sat next to them in the pews; Tipples the cat was content enough, curled up on the lap of Mrs Tankard. The pub lady decided, sensibly, to keep her dog Slipper on a leash, which, Patch observed, was not a happy state of affairs for his friend the whippet, who he observed had a mournful look on his face, slumped on the floor – all because he was being forced to stay in the same place for more than 10 minutes.

'I've never known Slipper stay in the same spot long without him wanting to be somewhere else!' concluded Patch.

Further along the pews sat Mr and Mrs Tavy with Gorse; this time of the day, being lunchtime, all three would normally be seen in the Colliers' Arms but being Sunday it was 'their day off'.

Immediately in front of them were the Stefferson family accompanied by Socks and Flossie.

Flossie was wearing her 'best collar' while Socks had stubbornly refused to put his on for the occasion, meowing and flicking a defensive paw every time Freda attempted to wrap it around his neck.

Of course, in prime position – who else – on the front row, right next to the aisle with the best view of the altar, was Mrs Curtois-Pughs; sitting right to her, on a fluffy cushion – especially embroidered with his name stitched on in bold Gothic type – was the contemptible Archie. Patch growled at the sight of him; an action not unnoticed by Mistress Ma.

'Now you be a good dog, Our Patch,' said Ma, turning to her pet. 'I don't want any trouble today, boy.'

Patch looked up at his adored mistress with a look that an angel would have been proud to possess. As Ma turned to adjust an out of place lock of hair on her daughter's head, Patch turned his attention to the organist to the right side of the altar. There was Mrs Popplethwaite, festooned in her questionably Sunday finest of a twin-set in imperial purple; to top off the outfit she sported a bonnet with two pheasant feathers poking out at a bizarre angle – ready to assault any unsuspecting soul that approached too near.

'I pity any poor bird nesting in that,' thought the terrier.

Mrs Popplethwaite, as she did every Sunday at this time, was sat on her stool warming up her instrument in anticipation of the start of the service.

Sitting on an adjacent organ stool, next to his podgy mistress, perched comfortably and looking very pleased with himself, was Genghis. Again Patch growled and again Mistress Ma gave him a disapproving look so the little dog was silent once more – Patch just growled 'inside' to himself instead at the sight of Hillthorpe's most loathsome creature.

'What's Genghis doing here?' he thought. 'I didn't think he worshipped the Great Bedlington in the Sky like the rest of us creatures!'

The 'Mongolian monster' was in fact ready to pounce in case any church mouse was brave, or foolish, enough to make an appearance from behind the skirting board. They weren't, not with Genghis there – even though there was an 'unwritten agreement', acknowledged by all the animals in Hillthorpe, that for this special service within the confines and holy sanctuary of the chapel a 'truce' was declared and 'no claw, paw or jaw' would harm a fellow creature.

All the animals honoured this sacred truce up to now but

it just showed how the mice and rats distrusted Genghis that they kept a respectful distance and listened and joined in to the service out of sight of their fellow creatures.

Proceedings began with the Reverend Sedgwick welcoming 'man, woman, child and beast' to the special service and introducing the first hymn – 'Blessed creatures one and all.'

In the hands of any other organist it was a relatively straightforward, delightful tune to play but in the care of Mrs Prudence Popplethwaite – encumbered with her sausage size fingers ('did someone say sausages' – as Patch's ears pricked) the well-known hymn became not so well recognised, as the congregation struggled to follow and match the notes being 'played' by the organist.

For some of those unfortunate animals present, with more sensitive hearing on the higher notes, it was all too much, and this was not helped by Slipper and Growler, who began to howl with indignation, which just added to the cacophony of noise.

'Their howling has more harmony than old two feathers,' thought Patch.

'Mrs Popplethwaite's playing is as flat as one of her Yorkshire puddings,' whispered Victor, a bit too loud, to his elder brother,' and all the Wagstaffs laughed – even Ma, who pretended to admonish her middle son by giving him a gentle slap on his head.

The Reverend Sedgwick was well known by both local clerics and his congregation for mixing his Methodist service with elements of the more orthodox traditions. As he blessed all in attendance with 'holy water' he took great delight in going up and down the aisle using his aspergillum to great effect and sprinkling or 'casting the waters' to bless 'man and beast' alike.

Unfortunately for one of the beasts, a few of the precious drops went straight into its left eye and an unsuspecting Archie jumped up from his, up to then, comfy spot on the cushion, and whimpered in protest at this affront – much to the consternation of Mrs Curtois-Pughs and much to the amusement of a delighted Patch. However, this pleasurable moment for the little terrier turned to displeasure when Archie's owner immediately placated her pooch with a big cuddle and a big biscuit treat to pacify her 'baby'. Having made the most of the situation and making sure he was the centre of attention once again, Archie returned to his luxurious cushion and deemed the service 'may continue'.

Reverend Sedgwick cleared his throat after the embarrassment and began his sermon, reminding his 'captive audience' of Luke, chapter 12, verse 6: 'Are not five sparrows sold for two cents? Yet not one of them is forgotten before God.'

This affirmation certainly caused a flutter with Cyril Pilcher's homing pigeons who cooed in veneration from their basket. It was 'the message' that Cyril had been waiting for and he resolved to have an extra 'flutter' himself at the next pigeon race.

The Reverend continued: 'Indeed, the very hairs of your head are all numbered. Do not fear; you are more valuable than many sparrows.'

This brought a nudge into Edward's ribs from Victor, who 'whispered' a little too loudly to his younger brother:

'If that's the case, God can't love Mr Hodgson, the smithy, very much, 'ee's bald as a coot!'

This brought a ripple of tittering from the Wagstaff siblings which came to an abrupt end when Ma gave a disapproving look and put her fingers to her lips.

After the sermon, however, it was during that popular hymn 'All Things Bright and Beautiful, All Creatures Great and Small' when the service took an even less harmonious course.

It was during this hymn that Patch, who up to then had been patiently sitting in the pew between Tommy and little Emma, decided 'to stretch his paws'.

Tommy let Patch go as he did not want to make a fuss in the middle of the hymn. 'Besides,' he assured himself, 'what harm could Patch do?'

. . . 'All things wise and wonderful, the Lord God made them all . . .'

Patch made his way down the side of the aisle, out of sight of most of the congregation; the people who could see him took no notice as they valiantly sang along to the hymn – despite the musical accompaniment.

He headed toward the organ until he could see Mrs Popplethwaite in full throttle, knocking the wind out of the poor, defenceless instrument. She pumped the pedals and pounded the keys with all the finesse of an angry baker pummelling and kneading dough or a boxer in training, battering a punch bag. What made it even worse for Patch was the self-proclaimed 'organist' compounded the din by adding her not so genteel voice to the proceedings. Patch once again winced and pinned back his ears to protect his hearing, struggling to decide which was worse – Mrs Popplethwaite's playing or her singing?

'There's not a cat's whisker between them,' he thought.

As Patch turned the corner of the aisle, there before him was a sight that brought all his mischievous nature to the fore and the little terrier thanked the 'Great Bedlington in the Sky' for such a 'heaven sent' opportunity.

'. . . *Each little flower that opens, each little bird that sings. . .'* trilled the assembly led by Mrs Popplethwaite.

For there in front of Patch, with his back to him and enthroned on his own organ stool, was the odious Genghis – unbelievably to Patch, although it had one evil eye scanning the horizon for any mouse movement, it was obviously enjoying the wailing and flaying of his mistress, because, unlike the rest of the congregation, the cat was purring along with her music, its tail swinging from side to side in disharmony with the tune.'

'He made their glowing colours, he made their tiny wings. . .'

Yes, Patch was aware of the 'unwritten truce' of 'no claw, paw or jaw will harm a fellow creature' but surely, he reasoned, 'this opportunity must be heaven sent by the Great Bedlington in the Sky himself' and 'on behalf of all the animals in Hillthorpe intimidated by the Mongolian monster – vengeance is mine,' said Patch to himself, as the temptation of Genghis' swinging tail proved too much to resist.

As the congregation belted out. . .

'All things bright and beautiful, all creatures great. . .'

It was at that very moment that the little terrier sunk his

teeth into Genghis' tail with the biggest 'Bedlington bite' he could muster.

'. . . *and small, all things bright and beautiful, The Lord God made them all.*'

The effect was almost immediate, as Genghis screeched out a high note never before heard, then or since, in Hillthorpe Chapel. Even Mrs Popplethwaite herself might have been in fervent admiration if she had the chance!

For Genghis, taken completely by surprise by the attack on his rear, leapt in terror and 'flew' from his stool with considerable force as he was propelled forward at speed, with claws fully extended, to land on the ample right arm of his unfortunate owner and knock her flying off her seat.

The music came to an unfortunate, or some would say 'fortunate', end as the bellows gasped out in merciful relief, their dying breath before they finally expired with a defiant rattle.

It also provided the perfect musical accompaniment for the congregation to witness the unforgettable sight of Mrs Popplethwaite lying on her back on the church floor with one leg raised fully in the air, arms flailing, inelegantly astride her organ stool with her skirt lifted to expose her undercarriage.

For a poor, shocked William Pickles, the nine-year-old in the front row, it was a sight that left a lasting impression – his mother later complained to Reverend Smethick, 'that her little Willy was still having nightmares for days after.'

Genghis, still wailing in pain, ran from pillar to post, altar to apse, in sheer terror and his panic spread like a bush fire to the other animals, who, up to then, were as relatively contented as a menagerie of animals could be in a confined space.

Slipper, of course, was the first, 'metaphorically and phorically' off the leash. The sound of Genghis screeching to the rafters and the sight of the feline, in fear and pain, dashing around dementedly in every direction, brought all of the whippet's natural instincts to the fore.

The combination of a demented Genghis and the wild unpredictability of an untethered Slipper bouncing off the aisles in a frenzy, like two loose cannons fired into the decks of a 17th century man-of-war, caused pandemonium amid the ranks of the congregation of Hillthorpe Chapel – humans and animals alike. Their actions sparked a veritable stampede.

One of the first victims was Archie, the spoiled spaniel, who was sent tumbling off his cushioned perch by his mistress, Mrs Curtois-Pughs, as she fell on him after the cross-eyed Slipper bolted into her legs; she winced in pain before sitting down at some speed, her ample rear unwittingly half crushing her beloved pet.

Archie responded with an even higher pitched shriek and in his sudden state of unmitigated fear, after being nearly crushed or smothered by the backside of his mistress, leapt free only to sink, in fright, his teeth into the rear of the unfortunate nearby ass, Dolly.

Dolly let out the loudest 'ee-aw' known to donkey kind and bucked her rear legs in protest at the indignation of having a canine's canines sunk into her buttocks. Her powerful hooves jerked violently through the nearest oaken pews, shattering them to smithereens, like the aforementioned cannon fire, into the timbers amidships.

The normally docile Dolly then proceeded to charge forward, 'ee-awing' as she went, before headbutting the unfortunate Reverend Smethick, who was catapulted over the font at a rate of knots, spilling its waters over the floors before the altar. Immediately Mrs Smethick, in attempting to rush to her husband's aid, lost her footing on the slippery surface, trying to avoid a disorientated rabbit, who had in the commotion hopped from its owner's grasp and appeared suddenly under her feet. She, too, soon found herself prostrate inelegantly on the floor next to her husband.

Panic quickly spread through the ranks of the congregation, especially among the animals who, up to then, had abided in an uneasy truce.

Jess the Labrador was next to break ranks after Dolly's powerful, bucking hoof had missed her by a proverbial whisker. She backed up with four paws nervously into her aisle mate Tipples, who in turn, leapt for her life in fear and straight onto the top of the basket of Cyril Pilcher's homing pigeons, uncoupling its catch and releasing its occupants into the air before their startled owner could react. The flock of birds began to flap around wildly all over the chapel of chaos, forcing people to duck as they fluttered around in a frenzy.

Worse was to come. All the vibrations caused by the furore only had the effect to unnerve all the rodent population, who began to scamper in terror through every available crack and hole to seek 'sanctuary' in the chapel.

Their sudden appearance was too much for every moggy in the village and nature now took its course. . . the 'temporary truce' was ended and the 'inner beast' exposed.

Socks and the normally dilatory Flossie did not know

which mouse to chase, their eyes never having seen such a flurry of furry rodents before. Gorse pursued the tail of the nearest rat he could find, not exactly knowing what to do, though, when he actually caught one.

However, it was not just the animal kingdom that suffered injury and indignation. The human toll was just as heavy.

In her haste to protect her 'ward' Jess, Molly the Alsatian had leapt from the pew and, intending to rush to her friend's side, only managed to land her full weight on the back of an unfortunate Mrs Fishwick.

Mrs Fishwick had only just recovered some of her dignity after the humiliation of recently witnessing, in public, her husband on top of a bedecked Mrs Popplethwaite in the butcher's shop during Patch's infamous sausage escapade. Now she found herself in a similarly embarrassing position as Molly's not inconsiderable bulk pushed her on top of Mr Hardwick, the ironmonger. The roles were definitely reversed, as it was now Mr Fishwick's turn to see his wife on top of the opposite sex – somehting that he secretly was grateful for as his wife had been reminding him for weeks about his 'embrace' with that dreadful Prudence Popplethwaite.

Tipples, the pub cat, sensibly seized the opportunity to lick from the floor the wine which was spilled from a knocked over chalice.

Soon Tipples became 'tiddly' and it was not the little cat's greatest moment when it later threw up over the two pheasant feathers sticking out from Mrs Popplethwaite's nearby bonnet, which had been earlier jettisoned on the floor.

Mrs Popplethwaite herself, after being assaulted by her beloved Genghis, managed, via the altar rail, to scramble to her feet; still coming to terms with the 'horrors' of her situation. She then picked up her precious Sunday bonnet, which Dolly had already stomped on in his fright and battered into an unrecognisable pulp.

Mrs Popplethwaite staggered towards Mrs Curtois-Pugh in the hope of a sympathetic ear and a word of comfort from her near social equal. However, the latter's attention was fully focused on reassuring her 'sweet little' Archie, who she had scooped into her protective arms to cradle, baby fashion, and to comfort and coo at him repeatedly in reassurance.

This reassurance was not helped when a 'coo' of another nature was heard above the chief clerk's wife and her whimpering and quivering pet, before a dollop of pigeon dropping was delivered straight into Archie's eye – the one that had not been previously 'blessed' with holy water!

In almost harmonious syncopation a cry or howl of despair emanated from both mistress and mutt.

Amid all the confusion and upset, Patch observed the shameful scene perched in his pew betwixt his Young Master and his Mistress. Throughout, he was a statue of calm personified.

The Wagstaffs were as shocked as their fellow congregation members at the scene, which now resembled as if an earthquake or whirlwind had descended upon the village chapel. Or as one more fervent ecclesiastical member had opined – 'an Act of God, for the sins of the village.'

It was not often that Ma praised 'Our Patch', as she showed her love in many small ways, but the little Bedlington's heart beamed with pride when she patted him on the tuft on top of his head and said to him: 'There, Our Patch, you've been the best behaved animal in this chapel today and that's a fact.'

Patch observed the shameful scene perched in his pew.

A proud Patch looked up at his object of adoration as if in a state of beatification – innocence personified as he looked 'doe-eyed' to return the loving look of his beloved Mistress.

As for Mrs Popplethwaite, her humiliation was not yet fully complete.

Despite the screams of several ladies whose sanity had temporarily left them due to the abundant presence of many rats and mice scampering at speed around the aisles, up, over on and under the pews and altar, the now focused Reverend Sedgwick, along with Ma Wagstaff, tried to restore some sort of order to the pandemonium surrounding them.

Mrs Popplethwaite, in still evident distress and undress, approached the Reverend and his wife and a few of the church seniors who had gathered hastily for a 'damage assessment' conference at the steps of the altar.

Still in a state of evident shock and partly resuscitated by a quick intake of smelling salts that she secreted in her clothing for such an occasion, Mrs Popplethwaite managed to voice:

'I… I… don't know what has possessed my Genghis; he's normally such a docile, sweet, well behaved little cat,' she gasped to the astonished assembly.

'I think the problem is, Mrs Popplethwaite,' came the immediate and clearly irritated voice belonging to Mrs Sedgwick, surveying the chaos around her, 'that your Genghis is obviously possessed by the Devil. . . It ought to be exorcised,' she said as she glared at the mistress of the Mongolian monster, who was in no doubt, in her mind, responsible for the near apocalyptic scene in the village chapel.

Mrs Popplethwaite, her hackles instantly raised by the

tone and blatant high handed accusation of the preacher's wife, sprang to the defence of her precious pet, like a lioness protecting her cub.

'I think...' she announced, rallying her composure and instinctively defending her pride... 'I think my Genghis has had plenty of exercise for one day, thank you, Mrs Sedgwick!'

With that she raised herself to her full 5 feet 1 inch stature, turned on her heels and headed in the direction of the chapel door, adjusting her battered bonnet and pulling up and dusting off her dress with her hands as she went, heading for the exit.

It was a 'mistressly' performance, like a queen of the ocean liner, weighing anchor and departing port, leaving all in her wake.

As for Genghis, he was not seen for five days before he came home scratching at his door and found by his mistress, undernourished, fur matted and soaked to the skin.

It was fully another two generations before another animal service was held again at Hillthorpe Chapel.

That evening Patch was given an extra sausage for, as Ma put it, 'his exemplary behaviour' that day in the chapel.

14

Odds on Slipper

AFTER much anticipation and preparation, the most important day in the district's social calendar had finally arrived. May 1, 1914 was a date that everyone in the village and the surrounding district had looked forward to, as it was the day of the Hillthorpe and Daleswick Annual Miners' Gala – a combination of sporting events, fun fair and merry making, with the emphasis on 'merry'.

May Day was one of the few national holidays which everyone in the little North Yorkshire mining community enjoyed, when the drudgery and darkness for most who worked both above and below the ground was forgotten; the grime wiped off all the faces and everybody, of all ages – on this rare occasions – were attired in their 'Sunday best'.

The annual extravaganza took place in three fields belonging to Farmer Ramsden; the gracious farmer consented, at no cost to the community, to his land being used to host a range of activities to entertain the village population and those who had crossed 'hill and dale' to be there that spring day.

In the sporting arena there were highly competitive games

with the tug-of-war, Cornish and arm wrestling bouts, boxing and athletics. Perhaps the most eagerly awaited encounter was the annual 'football' match between the Hillthorpe and Daleswick miners – played, unlike the rest of the games, on the 'slag heap' – where no holds were metaphorically, and in reality, barred in the quest for victory and a year's bragging rights. Many a participant incorporated the tactics that some of them had already employed in the wrestling or boxing earlier in the day.

For the first time in four years it was the men of Hillthorpe who triumphed 2-1 thanks to a late goal from Jethro Toon, the colliery fireman, who not without aid of knee and elbow to throw off the attentions of the Daleswick defenders, rose to head the ball from a corner kick to nod the winner past the flailing visiting goalkeeper. What followed was the inevitable punch-up between the teams – 'inevitable' as each side were encouraged by the partisan crowd of their supporters, who not only expected – nay demanded – a 'scrap' at the final whistle. They would have been greatly disappointed without some sort of confrontation or the chance to join in themselves. It was, to some, a 'rite of passage' for many a Hillthorpe and Daleswick lad, to at least come away with a 'shiner', or even two. It took the considerable and divine skills of Rev Sedgwick and a contingent of North Yorkshire Constabulary to restore order.

However, peace was only properly restored when local magistrate and mine superintendent Mr Beaulieu intervened with a loud hailer and threatened to remove the special licence of the Colliers' Arms that day 'unless fighting ceased forthwith.' Fighting ceased forthwith!

The Hillthorpe XI victory had left young Tommy Wagstaff

in excellent spirits – the exact opposite to those of his best pal, Bert Dyson, a passionate Daleswick supporter.

However, the 'big match' was not the only important issue decided that day. Neither was the Miners' Gala restricted to intense competition on the sporting field. Many a deep rivalry, and some say grudging respect, for your 'opponent' was unearthed in the horticulture tent, where colliers showed the 'fruits' of their labours from their allotments to vie for the 'Grand Rosette' – awarded each year to the entrant who had the most combined points in the vegetable section. Da Wagstaff was certainly a contender with his prowess, especially on the rhubarb, cabbage and potato front – aided by Patch, of course, who helped to make sure his master's prized entries were well watered and fertilised.

Of course, no miner's gala would be complete without the stirring sounds of the brass band – cornet, pipe and drum working in harmony to provide the perfect musical backdrop to the day. The miners were proud of their tuneful skills – ones which were handed down from 'father to son' – and drawn from the community's need to provide its own entertainment. Normally in district competitions there was great rivalry between the village colliery bands; however tradition had it that at the Hillthorpe and Daleswick Miners' Gala the two bands played together with their respective band leaders each taking the baton throughout the day's recitals.

Perhaps the quietest place of all on the day was a marquee erected by the men of the King's Own Yorkshire Regiment. Six soldiers, looking smart in their uniforms, were on hand to talk to potential recruits, but the only real interest came from young boys eager to hold a rifle or bayonet as there were few young men willing to take the 'King's shilling'.

The recruiting sergeant, a veteran of the Boer War, with his regulation ramrod back, barrel chest and impressive moustache, was perhaps the 'unmerriest' man at the gala that day, knowing his captain would not be pleased about the 'recruiting results' at one of North Yorkshire's premier gatherings – miners were normally a rich seam of new blood for the Army, but not today!

The sergeant stood upright with meaty hands clasped behind his back and a deep frown on his face as he surveyed the lack of activity in his tent – no doubt wishing he could employ the tactics of the Royal Navy in times of yore and merely 'press gang' his 'volunteers'.

He looked over with irritation up to the top field, where, in contrast to the comparable silence of the recruiting marquee, a sizeable and increasingly vocal crowd had gathered.

Two of the most eagerly anticipated events on the local canine calendar were to be 'unleashed' that day, within one hour of each other – the Hillthorpe and Daleswick whippet and course races.

Patch had decided to take young Master Tommy, along with his two paw pal Bert, so that they could bark their encouragement to his best doggy friend, Slipper. Of course, Patch could have taken part himself, even though he wasn't a whippet, but even he knew he could not outrun Slipper and besides, reasoned the Bedlington, 'I never like to be second in anything.'

For some unknown reason, Slipper's owner, the Colliers' Arms landlord Arthur Tankard, had great faith in his cross-eyed canine. It was a confidence that, it has to be said, was mostly misplaced, as Slipper's racing capabilities, had in previous meets, less than met its owner's expectations in terms of results.

The amiable Slipper was a 'conundrum' not only to his master but to the rest of the racing community in the district – the pencil thin whippet certainly had the speed and stamina but his sense of direction, lack of discipline and impatience was a constant source of bemusement and puzzlement to all. Obviously the handicap of being slightly cross-eyed did not help but as far as Arthur Tankard was concerned Slipper had all the qualities of a 'top dog', if only he could be pointed in the right direction – practically as well as metaphorically!

'I don't reet understand thee, Arthur,' puzzled Da, a good friend of the landlord. 'Yer not a man normally given to making rash decisions like, when it comes to money, you bein' a pub landlord, but when it comes to your Slipper yer let thy heart rule thy 'ead. Yer must 'ave lost a few bob to Uneven in the past couple of years.'

'Uneven' Stevens was the local bookmaker, known to all those foolish enough to partake in his 'trade' as a man 'short on odds and long in pockets,' as well as being 'a nasty bit of work'.

It was true what the landlord was being accused of by his friend and it lay uncomfortably with him but something 'nagged' inside him that 'Our Slipper will come good one day.'

Of course, Arthur had to walk a fine line in answering his 'nagging' inner voice, balanced against another more worldly one, the wrath of Mrs Tankard.

'The great Blondin 'imself would 'ave an easier time walkin' across the Niagara Falls on a tightrope,' lamented Arthur to Da, 'than me explainin' to my Mrs 'ow I lost any more money on our Slipper.'

It was a dilemma for any landlord to cry in his cups.

But Arthur Tankard was not a man who would not 'put his money where his mouth was' and whenever asked by any of his clients at the Colliers' Arms or by a fellow member of the racing community: ''Ow's yer Slipper goin' to do in the next race, man?' Arthur would invariably reply, without hesitation, 'Eh, our Slipper is goin' to be first past the post, no fret lad.'

His confidence in his pet, however, was not shared by anyone but himself when it came to placing a bet on racing day.

'Slipper could be the fastest whippet in the whole of the Ridings,' enthused its owner to Da Wagstaff one night, while pulling a pint of stout, 'if only 'e knew where 'e was suppose to be goin'!'

''E's a winner alright Joe, is our Slipper. I knew it the first time I saw 'im as a puppy when I bought 'im from a traveller for a firkin of ale. I think Slipper must 'ave a bit of Romany 'imself in 'im cos he can never settle in one place for more than a minute. But I know that dog has potential. I just know it Joe!'

'Aye, if only it could be harnessed,' replied a sympathetic Da, a man not without some fine judgement when it came to the animal kingdom – especially in the homing pigeon department, and as Patch himself would have naturally concurred, a man of impeccable foresight in choosing a fine specimen of man's best friend!

Now if there was one 'dead cert' that Uneven Stevens could guarantee at any race, it was that Slipper Tankard would be the first dog out of the trap and the last dog over the line – if, in fact, the wandering whippet ever reached the finishing line. There was one infamous occasion when for some mysterious reason the amiable Slipper, with the scampering pack well behind him, turned around in mid race past his fellow competitors and bolted back over the starting line in the opposite direction after he heard his pal Patch bark 500 yards away; with his tongue hanging out and tail wagging Slipper headed off to join his friend, to, in his mind, 'see what Patch wuz up to.'

However, even with the constant haranguing by Arthur's wife, who used to give her husband a right 'ear bashin' when he came back from the races empty pocketed, it did not stop him repeating the same mistake race after race.

'We would be retired by now if it weren't for yer Slipper,' berated Mrs Tankard. 'Yer spend more money on that daft dog than yer do on me, Arthur Tankard. I don't know who's more doolally – you, our Slipper or me for puttin' up with both of yer useless creatures.'

It wasn't just the canines of Hillthorpe who occasionally found themselves in the doghouse!

But Arthur Tankard remained dogmatic that 'his Slipper had what it takes'. He knew his 'boy' was the fastest in the district and 'that dog 'as more natural energy than the sun itself', he reasoned.

'Slipper is far faster than Panther (a dark grey whippet belonging to Amos Riley) who wins most of the races around Hillthorpe and Daleswick,' thought Arthur. 'My Slipper is a natural, 'e just needs pointing in the right direction.'

It was an ironic thought, with more than a slither of truth to describe Arhur Tankard as North Yorkshire's 'unluckiest' whippet owner and one of the sport's most impecunious punters, when it came to actually winning a bet.

In fact, true to form, Slipper, much to the frustration of the

Colliers' Arms' landlord, lived up to his reputation with the betting fraternity in the gala's whippet race. This was a straight 'let off the lead' sprint across the field.

Uneven Stevens, eager to keep such a lucrative loser as Arthur Tankard, always had a 'sympathetic ear' when the landlord approached him to place his latest bet. Every race Skipper took part in the unscrupulous bookie always offered 'special odds' to its owner – perhaps 9 to 2 compared to 4 to 1 to the rest of his clientele. The bookmaker knew Arthur could not resist the temptation and a sly, lop-sided grin spread across his face when the latter looked the former straight in the eye and informed him: 'Yer mark my words Mr Stevens, my Slipper will show yer 'e's a winner, yer'll see!'

The bookie tried hard to restrain his glee but could not help exhaling a short snort of satisfaction, not unnoticed by the punter.

But Arthur could not read Uneven's thoughts which at the moment were: 'There's as much chance as Sunderland winning the league and cup double or Emily Pankhurst being invited to join a Masonic Lodge as Slipper winning the field dash!'

The unfortunate truth for Arthur Tankard was that the more he insisted on Slipper's racing capabilities the more he was determined to win his bet; the more he lost, the more he had to make up for, and each time the wily bookie offered just slightly better odds to entice the not so wealthy landlord to chance another bet. It was a vicious circle.

Indeed, if there was a bet on Slipper chasing his tail, Arthur Tankard would have a flutter on it and the result would have been the same – with Arthur losing a sum of money and the bookie pocketing the same amount; the daft dog being distracted and ending up chasing its own nose!

So it proved in the Gala's field dash. There were eight dogs – with Panther, the alpha dog, once again the favourite; there were three other strong contenders, Chaser, Bingo and Flash. Making up their numbers were Likely Lad, Moonbeam and Wandering Star, as well, of course, with Slipper the rank outsider to all but its ever deluded owner.

''Ere Arthur,' offered Da Wagstaff to an obviously nervous pub landlord before the race, 'that Wandering Star would be a more proper name for your Slipper!' It didn't help put his friend at ease.

Arthur, in fact, didn't respond to the well intentioned comment, which Da hoped would bring the whippet owner some much needed light relief. No, Arthur continued to brush down his dog – a difficult task as he had to brush and hold onto the animal who was straining to get away. For some reason the landlord was convinced that hard brushing his dog at the last possible moment would get rid of any unwanted hairs, which, in turn, would mean a decrease in weight and an increase in speed!

As the crowds gathered to watch the start, Uneven Stevens was accompanied by a rather tall, muscular, young man with huge cauliflower ears, evidence of the many fights he had been involved in during his 'career'. The unsavoury characters homed in to the pub landlord, relishing the opportunity of extracting some easy cash.

'Hello Arthur, it's a pity your Slipper isn't as good a runner as he looks,' said Uneven, 'can't be easy a pub dog with all those slops going a beggin'. Perhaps that's why your dog can't hold a straight line – he enjoys his tipple too much!'

Uneven roared with laughter at his own 'joke' and having been given a poke by his boss with an unsubtle elbow in the ribs, 'Cauliflower', although quite uncertain what he was supposed to be laughing at, 'decided' to join in too.

''Course Arthur,' added the bookmaker, whose eyes narrowed now he was concentrating on the business end, 'Nine to two says your Slipper will win on the nose. 'Course these are generous odds but I've a reputation for being a fair and generous man.'

'Yeah, generous with other people's hard earned money,' interrupted a clearly annoyed Da, turning to his friend the landlord. 'Don't listen to 'im Arthur, yer only lose,' – a remark which caused offence to Cauliflower, who took a threatening step towards Da. Patch, sitting patiently by his master, omitted a low growl in protection, ready to spring into action if needed.

Uneven, sensing the atmosphere, grabbed the arm of his 'associate' and pretended to ignore Da's 'interfering advice' to one of his more easily manipulated clients. Patch resumed his seating position now the danger was allayed as Cauliflower duly took a step back.

'Naturally, if you want to withdraw your Slipper now, nobody would think any less of you as a whippet handler – perhaps you could take up breeding rabbits instead,' sniped Uneven, hoping to provoke a response.

With this suggestion Cauliflower sniggered before he and Uneven both burst out laughing at the thought.

''Course,' Uneven continued with a thin layer of understanding, 'a man of your standing in the community, Arthur, is good by me for credit. And if your Slipper is as good as yer be tellin' all the other owners I reckon £3 at 9 to 2 is more than generous odds. 'Course if your Slipper ain't good enough. . .'

Before he could finish and any other insult was added, Arthur interrupted, 'Make it three guineas,' he told the bookmaker, looking at him straight in the eye.

As quick as a flash Uneven spat on his palm and held out an outstretched hand to the landlord to seal the deal. Arthur, forlornly, raised his hand and shook to make 'the contract'.

Even more quickly Cauliflower opened out a large Gladstone bag full of notes and a healthy assortment of coinage from the already collected tote. Arthur reluctantly handed over the three pounds, a florin and the remains of his coppers by throwing them into the bag. Cauliflower smiled as he closed the money holder the instant the cash 'was in the bag'. Uneven took out a little black note book and with a pencil, produced as if by magic from behind his ear, he scribbled down the latest bet.

With the cash secured, Uneven and his muscular assistant moved on in search of their next 'victim'.

'We'll show 'em,' pouted Arthur. 'Slipper won't let me down. 'E's a winner is my boy.'

Patch looked up and gazed at his master, and his knowing stare was returned by Da; which communicated in language unknown, that both man and dog saw fit to shake their heads in disbelief, as if to say: ''E Arthur, ye must be soft in the 'ead.'

So it proved to be. Sure enough, at the beginning Slipper surged ahead, eager to be let off the lead at the starting pistol. Within no time he was five lengths ahead and gaining from Panther, who was edging out Flash for second spot. Arthur shouted his encouragement and even Patch yelped his from the sidelines but, true to form, Slipper stopped dead in mid tracks, with the finishing line, agonisingly for Arthur, firmly in sight and the race his for the taking. Instead, this time, the reason of his distraction, was that Slipper had decided to answer a sudden call of nature. He had stopped with a braking system that any clifftop lemming would have died for, and immediately started to sniff the ground. After circling the site three times, he then assumed a squat position and answered the call, as the pursuing pack sprinted by to the finishing line.

Arthur, on the sidelines, held his head in his hands in despair, knowing that he had not only lost a large sum of money but also that he had to explain his losses to Mrs Tankard – a task he was not looking forward to. He wasn't helped in his spirits when Cauliflower gave him a hearty slap on his back, the latter joining in the bonhomie of his boss, who shouted: 'Never mind, Arthur, always next time! The hare coursing's in an hour's time, see yer there,' as he and his associate continued in their merriment at the landlord's expense before they went off to find a private place to count their 'earnings' from the race.

Arthur called over his charge, and at the sound of his master's voice Slipper came galloping over, now much relieved, jumping on his master and giving him a friendly wet lick on the face – oblivious to Arthur's current gloom.

'Oh Arthur,' said Da, trying to console his friend on his latest betting loss, 'What 'ave yer done man?'

'Oh Slipper,' thought Patch, 'What 'aven't yer done!'

For Uneven Stephens his torment of the landlord of the Colliers' Arms was not over with yet, especially as 'only' three of Arthur's guineas were 'in the bag'. Oh no, the weaselly bookmaker sensed there was more 'sport' to derive from Arthur Tankard and certainly a few extra pounds to be made. Honing into people's weaknesses was one of Uneven's strengths, and besides, 'nobody was forced to gamble,' he reasoned. 'People always want somethin' for nothin'. They just get greedy, not content with what they got.'

Uneven fancied himself as a 'bit of a philosopher' and was never short of an informed opinion – uninformed as it was to any who had the misfortune to hear it.

'Let a punter think 'e's won a couple pennies and next time 'e'll bet a couple of shillings. Let 'im win a few bob and next thing you know 'e'll be layin' down a few quid,' was his reasoning.

'A couple of small wins and 'e thinks 'e's on a winning streak so 'e bets more on the next race. Then you got him! They never know when to stop, thank Gawd. They just get greedy.'

His philosophical thoughts and wisdom were offered to the nearby Cauliflower but unfortunately for their purveyor it just went through one of Cauliflower's cauliflower ears and out the other.

'That Arthur Tankard, 'e's just like all the rest – think 'e can beat the odds man.' continued Uneven. ''Ee'll be back, you just mark my words. 'Ee'll be back.'

Cauliflower stared at his toes in response; his job wasn't to think, he reasoned, he was there to collect the monies and offer his 'protection'.

However, contrary, to Uneven's prediction, Arthur Tankard had still not come to place his bet for the hare coursing so the bookmaker was at odds and wondered why he had not had the expectant enquiry from the landlord – who had never failed him in the past.

With only ten minutes to go before the race Uneven was

beginning to think Arthur was going to miss out on a bet – a situation he could not, and more importantly for his pocket, would not allow. Being a determined man Uneven 'philosophised' to himself that 'if Mohammed won't come to the mountain, then the mountain would go to Mohammed' – and off he trekked, with Cauliflower in toe, to track his prey.

Sure enough he found Arthur behind the steward's hut on the top field, grooming his 'steed' for the forthcoming hare coursing. Slipper stood there with his huge cross-eyes, eagerly scouring the field, with his big tongue flopping out to one side. He was, as always, itching to get away.

'Why Arthur, fancy bumping into you and your fine canine,' he boomed. 'I was just saying to my colleague, I wonder 'ow my good friend Arthur was after his near win at the last race.'

Turning to his minder, he added: ''Course I've never seen anything so unfortunate in me racing life, 'ave you Cauliflower?'

Cauliflower gave a puzzled look, not sure what misfortune had befallen the punter, apart from losing his money again.

'Your Slipper looked a dead cert Arthur,' continued Uneven. 'I've never seen such an untimely call of nature just when this wonderful whippet had the race in the bag.

'You must be down in the dumps, man.'

The phrase 'down in the dumps' was not one Arthur wanted to think of at that particular moment!

To reinforce his 'empathy' Uneven bent down to give the dog a friendly pat on the head, but Slipper, usually a friendly creature, let out a low growl.

Arthur looked slightly embarrassed by his dog's unusual reaction as the bookmaker quickly pulled his hand away.

Instead, to cover his awkwardness at this snub, Uneven moved across to Arthur to patronisingly pat him on the back instead.

'If your Slipper had only gone a few more lengths yer would 'ave won a pile – 'e was steaming ahead!'

Again this was a very unnecessary choice of words, given Arthur's recent racing predicament, but these clever comments went completely over the head of his intended victim and were even further away from being comprehended in their intent by Cauliflower.

Uneven feigned sympathy towards Arthur but inside he laughed to himself at his own 'humorous' observations.

''Course Arthur, I felt sorry for yer in the circumstances and feel very bad how close yer were to such a deserved victory. As you know, I make a modest livin' as a turf accountant, Arthur,' he expounded, rocking slightly on his Cuban heels for more effect. He tugged on the lining of his tweed jacket. 'My heart goes out to punters like you, Arthur, who everyone in Hillthorpe and Daleswick know as a true sportsman.

'I tell yer what I'm going to do man. I'm going to give your Slipper the more than generous odds of 12 to 1 in the hare coursing, just to redress the balance, so to speak. Yer can't say fairer than that man, can yer?'

At the conclusion of these words he yet again patted Arthur, this time on the shoulder.

A clearly annoyed Arthur muttered: 'I 'ain't bettin',' still raw over the loss of both a large sum of money and his reputation from the previous race.

'Come on, Arthur. I'm tryin' to do you a favour 'ere. . . Alright, look I'll give yer 13 to 1, can't say fairer,' offered the ever optimistic Uneven.

'I ain't bettin', can't afford it,' came the instant reply from the pub landlord.'

'That's right, don't listen to him, Arthur. You've lost enough today. Yer can't afford to lose anymore, man,' advised a concerned Da, whose wise counsel was appreciated and respected by the pub landlord.

Not to be put off, Uneven smiled or, more accurately, smirked, knowing that this 'fish' had to be reeled in slowly; he was up to the challenge.

Uneven, yet again, patted Arthur, this time on the shoulder as if saying 'there, there' to a confused child.

An increasingly irked Arthur muttered: 'I'll nae bet,' the previous race still raw to him.

'Come on Arthur. I'm trying to do you a favour 'ere.' Uneven hesitated calculatingly for effect to coax his prey.

'Alright, look I'll give you 14 to 1, can't say fairer than that,' offered the ever optimistic Uneven.

'I'll nae bet man. I can't afford it,' came the instant reply from the pub landlord. 'Lost too much last time, what will me Mrs say?'

'At those odds, Arthur,' came the quick and well-practised response from the bookmaker, 'you can't afford not to. Anyway, man, yer don't seem to be a man who's afraid of his Mrs. Maybe I got yer wrong, Arthur Tankard. Yer never strike me as the henpecked sort. 'Course, I didn't know yer 'ave to ask yer good lady's permission every time yer want a flutter. . .'

It was a low shot by Uneven but his gamble paid off, as Arthur was a proud man and this barbed comment by the bookmaker touched a nerve.

Arthur got off his haunches, rose to his full height and looked the stocky bookmaker straight in the eye.

'I'm not afraid of my Mrs and I don't need her permission for anythin' – not that I don't think the world of her and 'av the greatest respect like – but if yer ever say that to me again I'll knock yer block off, Mister Stevens.' He jabbed a fat finger into the bookies' shoulder. 'Yer can bet on that and write it in yer little black book!'

Uneven smiled but defensively took a step back, at the same time dramatically brushing away from his tweed jacket at the spot where Arthur's finger had touched.

The considerable bulk of Cauliflower stepped a couple of feet closer when seeing his boss 'threatened' – knowing that this usually was enough to put off any potential attacker.

However, the pub landlord had not finished and Uneven glanced at Cauliflower for reassurance concerning his physical welfare. It was not the first time the bookmaker had gone too far with one of his punters.

'Yer can patronise me, insult my Mrs and sneer at my dog, Mr Stevens but you know what – as God is my witness, I will wipe that smile off yer face and today's the day. I know it. I'll take yer bet. 20 to 1, did yer say? If yer man enuff, put me down for three quid.

Da intervened, seeing his friend rise to 'the bait'.

'Arthur. Don't do it, man. You can't afford to lose again. It's madness, especially with your Slipper.'

But his plea fell on deaf ears as now Arthur's blood was up – a state that the wily bookmaker had intended by his constant trickle of barbs.

'20 to 1,' exclaimed Uneven, a little taken aback by the normally meek Arthur's effrontery. '20 to 1,' he repeated for emphasis, 'I never offered those odds in my life and for three quid, that's an insult. I tell yer what Arthur, since you been up front with me. I'll give you 20 to 1, but you got to put on some real money. Say a tenner.'

Arthur's face ashened at such a thought but before he could tell Uneven to dismiss the idea as such an amount was totally beyond him, the wily bookmaker rubbed in the salt.

''Course, if you're not prepared to put your money where yer gob is,' smirked Uneven, smiling at Cauliflower and winking for added effect.

'And yer have to throw in Slipper. Give him to me. In proper hands that mutt could even win a race or two. At least I'll teach 'im to cross the finishing line.' With that Uneven and Cauliflower burst out in a heinous laugh but Arthur was not amused.

'Don't do it, Arthur,' repeated Da, this time with more desperation in his voice. 'Betting such a sum as £10 is one thing, man, but to bet your dog as well. 'E's more than a pet to you Arthur, and yer know it. Don't be soft in the 'ead. That man (pointing to Uneven) is the devil himself and you won't want to be owin' 'im nowt. No way man.'

It was true, but as sure as if he had drunk five pints of his own porter followed by a couple of whisky chasers – even though he was stone cold sober – Arthur's reasoning went completely out of the window. The sight of the bookie's malevolent and smirking face was like a red rag to a bull and there were some challenges a man could not turn down, if he could call himself a man, and this was such an occasion for Arthur Tankard.

He looked at Slipper and knew that a gauntlet had been thrown down.

'Where I'm going to get £10 and what am I doing betting on our Slipper,' thought Arthur, but reason and sentiment were not his strongest instincts at that moment and the bookie had hit a nerve deep within the landlord's soul itself.

He looked down at his dog, who attempted to return his gaze with his big cross-eyes, wagging his tail trustingly at his master.

'Yer on, £10 it is, on the nose at 20 to 1. I 'aven't got the money reet now but yer know I'll pay yer if I lose, but I'll swear to God this will be the last bet I will ever make or 'E upstairs can strike me down.'

'Oh, don't you fret, man,' replied Uneven, with more than a hint of menace. 'You will pay, Arthur Tankard, one way or the other. When yer lose, and yer will, if yer don't pay it, it won't be God striking you down, yer can be certain of that. It will be me.'

This was music to Cauliflower's ears and he let out a contented grunt at the future opportunity of carrying out his duties. He smiled to himself, thinking that 'Sometimes it was more fun when the punters didn't pay out.' He almost salivated at the prospect.

It was the second time that day that Da had uttered the words: 'Oh Arthur, what 'ave yer done man?' and shook his head in utter disbelief and bewilderment.

Even Patch, sat down on the grass beside his master, put his head between his paws and omitted a wearisome whine. Slipper though, just wagged his tail and stuck out his long tongue, oblivious to his coming fate.

Rumour soon spread as fast as Da releasing his homing pigeons on race day, or indeed, more pertinently, like the doors of the Colliers' Arms being swung open on a Saturday night, that Arthur Tankard had bet £20 and claim to his Slipper with Uneven Stephens.

There were heard one or two gasps among the sporting fraternity, especially among the racing dog owners, who could not believe such a previously unheard of amount was being chanced on such an unpredictable commodity as Slipper – a dog that for all his great potential had currently not succeeded in one victory during his 'racing' career.

''E must be mad,'; ''E must be barkin''; ''E must be a pint short of a gallon' – were just a few of the kinder comments, of those hearing of Arthur's contract with the bookie.

There were few who had a good word to say about Uneven Stephens, who's reputation for race rigging, short odds, money lending at extortionate rates (normally to those who owed him money due to a betting loss), and methods of 'collection' were universally despised throughout the North Yorkshire Riding.

'Yer can bet your bottom dollar that Uneven won't be payin' out on that one,' said one.

'Slipper's got as much chance of winning as Sunderland winnin' the double,' said another. 'Yer get better odds on my misses cookin' a decent Yorkshire puddin',' offered another brave race goer, earning a laugh from those around him and a jocular elbow in his ribs from a red-faced wife standing next to him.

All the banter about the annual hare coursing event at the gala only served to draw a bigger crowd than usual to the race. The more spectators the more Uneven Stephens took in bets – which just swelled his Gladstone bag even more – he having the monopoly of the tote due to other bookies being 'persuaded' not to compete on the big day.

It was certainly looking to be a profitable day for Uneven and his associate, with just one bet to go.

The hare coursing, as traditional at the Hillthorpe and Daleswick Annual Miners' Gala, was an open event – meaning that it was not just the whippets who could take part but any other dog whose owners fancied their chances. Thus there was a large 'field' of 28 assorted dogs, ranging from whippets, lerchers, greyhounds and terriers to a few mongrels, battling not just for the cash reward from the on course betting but also for the annual prized possession of the Herbert Halfacre trophy – named after its patron, a former mine owner in the area whose family fortunes from mining, due to gambling, had literally 'gone to the dogs'.

Among the canines was the not so betting favourite Slipper, who, unbeknown to him, had his very future hanging on the forthcoming event. Beside him was Patch, who had begrudgingly agreed to join in the race – sensing that it was a race he had a chance of victory in, being one that did not only require speed, a quality that he was not without as a Bedlington, but also one which needed skill and a little cunning – two natural attributes he took for granted as a representative of his breed.

There was a slight breeze in the air; a chilly north easterly blowing across the field as the owners and their charges began to try and form some sort of starting line up in the top field.

Cedric Hardcastle, the race marshal who was bedecked in a white coat that had seen better days, barked his orders through a loudhailer in one hand and held a white handkerchief in another.

The experienced marshal knew that trying to organise 'perfection' and order to the start of a hare coursing race was as useless as one man rounding up a flock of Wensleydales without a sheepdog.

So, without further ado, and a nod to his assistant Rollie Robinson, who had the job of releasing the hare from the sack, Cedric put the loudhailer to his lips, lifted the white handkerchief high above his head. He then uttered the magic words all the expectant crowd had been waiting for. 'On your marks and get set'. The owners had their equally excitable dogs, who were barking and pulling on their leads, eagerly awaiting his final instruction. As Cedric brought the handkerchief down and Rollie 'freed' the sacrificial hare, the marshal shouted 'Go' and the pandemonium ensued.

As the crowd flanking the course roared on their favourites and the owners eagerly encouraged their charges to do their duty, 25 dogs thrust in one direction in pursuit of their unfortunate quarry.

Quick 'out of the blocks' was Patch himself, keeping both eyes peeled on the small, blurred brown speedster in front of him, its four legs criss-crossing each other with every powerful stride. Tommy shouted, 'Go on Patch, go get him!', and even in the noisy mêlée Patch swelled with pride knowing that the eyes of two key members of his pack were upon him and hearing their encouragement only strengthened his resolve for glory.

While Patch led the whirlwind, which was the pack of 25 growling, snarling, bloodthirsty canines in pursuit of a poor defenceless creature, there was one other dog which had very different ideas.

When Arthur Tankard let his Slipper off the lead, true to form, it was off like a shot and even ahead of Patch himself just 10 yards into the race. With so much riding on Slipper's shoulders its owner felt a surge of excitement as his dog raced into the lead. He screamed after the whippet, urging him to pursue the hare who was making speedy progress across the field. Slipper had already gained a couple of lengths on his friend Patch, who himself, had half a length on the third placed Flash, closely followed by Bingo, with the rest of the pack closely bundled together snapping on the heels of the early leaders.

But then something extraordinary happened that evaporated any initial notions that Arthur Tankard had for victory in the most important race in his life. Instead of heading off in pursuit of the hare, which had turned to the right towards the top of the field, Slipper suddenly decided to turn sharp left and darted across the field in the opposite direction.

Even Patch could not believe it.

His game plan was to get to the hare first but not 'go for the kill' and then 'let' his best mate Slipper take the honours and at the same time keep off the other dogs to make sure his pal took the spoils – knowing how much was at stake for Slipper and his owner to win the race. Of course, Patch reasoned, he would have reminded Slipper many a time after the race, that it was he, Patch, who had really won it, having nobly sacrificed victory in the cause of his friend. Patch was not the sort of dog to hide his light under a bushel!

Patch had gone over his 'game plan' a few times with Slipper, just in case his not so bright pal did not understand his tactics. However, the Bedlington still could not believe his eyes when the whippet took the opposite direction to the rest of the pursuing pack. Patch did not even have time to bark at Slipper to get back into line.

'If ever a dog deserved an owner's slipper on his behind for sheer stupidity, it was Slipper,' thought Patch.

Arthur stood with the rest of the owners, in the middle of the field. His jaw dropped in incredulity as Slipper had done it again, seemingly snatching defeat from the jaws of victory. This time there was no escape for the unlucky landlord.

'Oh Slipper. 'Ow am I going to find £10 to pay that awful man Stevens?' he thought in despair. 'Not only that but they will take yer away boy and I'll never see yer again. Oh, how could I have been such a fool! Oh, God forgive me. I've been such a stupid, stupid man.'

Arthur sank to his knees with the enormity of it all, overcome with despondency. Da felt a lump rising in his throat at seeing his friend in such a pitiful state.

The depth of Arthur's despondency was only equalled by the delight of Uneven Stevens and his accomplice Cauliflower, who were observing proceedings with the throng of the crowd on the side of the field. Their smiles were as wide as the nearby River Ned at the expectancy of a bumper harvest seemingly 'in the bag' and the prospect of snatching the agile landlord's whippet to exploit at future races or sell on to a gullible punter.

But then, just as all seemed lost to the landlord of the Colliers' Arms, what can only be described as a 'minor miracle' took place on the top field of Hillthorpe village that May Day.

Slipper, for reasons known only to him and his Maker, decided to stop and sit, gasping for breath after his exertions near the top of the wall which enclosed the field – a full 120 yards away from the hare and its closing pack. After regaining his breath, Slipper investigated a tic which had been crawling on his shoulder and gave it a scratch with his rear left paw.

In the meantime, Patch at the other end of the field, was just about on the hare and began to close in for the kill, hotly pursued by the voracious pack. The hare, sensing that it was in immediate danger and faced with a granite wall too high to leap over, changed gear and sped along the base of the top of the wall, in the direction of the disorientated Slipper, who was more interested at the present in ridding himself of the tic and totally oblivious to the advancing quarry.

Without even knowing what was going on, Slipper, who happened to be yawning in response to his recent exertions, suddenly found, with exquisite timing, that the hare had dashed into his gaping jaws. The stunned Slipper was reeled over by the impact of the little hare hitting him at speed and with the 'wind knocked out of his sails' closed his jaws in automatic response, clamping it around the neck of the unfortunate buck, and killing it instantly.

If ever there was a case of 'if Mohammed won't go to the mountain, than the mountain will go to Mohammed' this was it!

The gobsmacked Slipper waved the carcass in the air a few times in an attempt to rid himself of the uninvited 'assailant' before throwing it away in disgust onto the ground. Immediately Patch and the rest of the pack dived in and pounced on the already dead hare and tore it to bloodied pieces but not before Cedric Hardwick had declared Slipper the winner on his loudhailer.

Arthur could not believe what he had just seen before his eyes. His Slipper had actually won! He leapt up in the air with delight. Did a jig and then raised high his arms to the skies before falling to his knees, this time in high excitement, before crying out to the heavens: 'Thank yer, God, thank yer God. It's a bloomin' miracle.'

The first to congratulate him was Da. 'I've never seen anything like it Arthur, that Slipper of yours is quite a dog. 20-1 Arthur, I reckon you could have got more like two million to one if you predicted the outcome of what's just happened. I'll never see anythin' like that again in my lifetime,' said Da, who was nearly as joyous and relieved as his friend the landlord.

Still in shock Arthur could only mutter to himself, 'My Slipper, I knew 'e 'ad what it takes. I knew it.'

The crowd went wild, their excitement and joy only adding to the sheer confusion of one very lucky, and about to be very much in profit, dog race owner.

Arthur was bursting with pride and gave the *Victor ludorum* such a big hug, that Slipper, who was a bag of bones anyway, was almost crushed, enveloped by a boa constrictor like grip.

The whippet, not realising the enormity of his achievements wriggled and 'bucked' – perhaps an unfortunate phrase in the circumstances – eager to be free. It was an unexpected big fat kiss on his forehead from his owner that did it – and the harassed dog found the extra impetus to evade Arthur's clutches.

Once out of the 'strait jacket' Slipper puffed and blew as he took in gasps of air to regain his breath. After this was accomplished he then suddenly screwed his face up and began to spit – to rid himself of the awful taste of hare hair and flesh which still lingered in his mouth.

The first dog to congratulate him was Patch, who, in true doggy fashion, pounced on his friend and pushed him over in celebration; when Slipper came out of the roll, Patch yelped at him with delight and the whippet responded by gleefully yelping back in acknowledgement before they sprung and gambolled all over the field in pure joy together.

Soon a fair size crowd had gathered mid-field with an embarrassed Arthur the centre of attention. Da slapped him on the back, and this time the pub landlord enjoyed the friendly gesture.

'Eh Arthur. I'm so chuffed for thee, it couldn't 'ave 'appened to a grander lad. Yer showed 'em; you and that daft dog Slipper of yours.'

'I still can't believe it, Joe,' replied Arthur with tears in his eyes. 'Our Slipper, a winner at last. If 'e never wins another race again that dog will always be a winner with me!'

'That's the spirit, Arthur,' continued Da. 'Yer 'ad your miracle today. Take yer money and never bet again lad – it's a mug's game and yer know it!'

'Aye Arthur,' nodded the publican. 'I know. I learned my lesson today. Yer know me Joe, I'm not a religious man – I'm a pub landlord and we're not known for our chapel going, particularly as the church puts a dampener on any Sunday profits, but I promise you this, Joe Wagstaff' – and as he did so Arthur looked his friend firmly in the eye – I gave my pledge to Him above today that if our Slipper was victorious I will never bet again. I've seen the light!'

Da laughed.

'I believe yer Arthur, but the only light yer see man is ale that comes in a bottle. But I believe yer, 'cause I wouldn't want to be in your boots, Arthur Tankard, if you broke yer promise.

'In fact, I'll take 20-1 that you get struck down by lightnin',' before adding for jovial emphasis, 'Nay, lad, 30-1 says two bolts of lightning.'

Arthur and Da both chuckled at that one and Tommy, standing next to his father, could not remember seeing Da laugh so much in his life and he too joined in the merriment.

But their bonhomie was not shared by all who were congregated on the top field of Farmer Ramsden's farm at that moment. While Arthur, Da and Tommy, along with the assembled members of the Hillthorpe and Daleswick Racing Dogs fraternity, enjoyed the talk about the spectacle and even more, the unexpected result, there were two very flustered figures, only twenty yards away, who were not joining in the celebrations.

Uneven Stevens was incandescent with rage and if ever a human being was capable of spitting feathers, then it was the loathsome bookmaker at that moment.

Cauliflower, eager to be 'in tune' with his master, sensed the indignation emanating from Uneven's whole demeanour at such an 'unfair' result.

The pair looked at the jubilant scene across the field, which only added to their sense of loss and discomfort.

'If yer think you've won the race with that stupid mutt of yours Arthur Tankard, then yer've got another thing comin',' muttered the bookie under his breath to himself. 'This is not over, not by a long chalk!'

Poking Cauliflower with a sharp elbow in the ribs Uneven gave his orders.

'Come on, let's see about who really won this race,' he spat, and he proceeded at a rapid pace toward Cedric Hardcastle, the race marshal. Close on his heels came Cauliflower, frantically clutching the precious Gladstone bag, which was almost bursting at its seams.

But as he took as big a stride as his stumpy legs could manage, Uneven's temper began to cool as his natural guile started to set in.

'Now Cedric, that was quite a race wasn't it?' was his opening gambit. 'I've never seen such entertainment – how you managed to attract a field of such top talent I'll never know.'

For added dramatic effect he turned to Cauliflower as an unwitting 'sounding board' as he continued.

'Why, I was just saying to my associate here, this must be the best organised dog race in the whole of North Yorkshire, didn't I, Mr Nightingale?' He then gave Cauliflower a stern but expectant stare to elicit the right response. The mention of his real name took Cauliflower by surprise.

'Aye. . . aye,' stuttered Cauliflower, not quite fully comprehending what right response was expected of him but still making an uneducated guess – which, thankfully for him, turned out to be the right one.

His apparent successful answer emboldened him so he added: 'Yeah, if not the 'hole of Yorkshire, Mr Stevens.'

It was the right reply. Uneven gave a lopsided grin and continued to engage the race marshal.

'And I must say, Mr Hardcastle,' while patting him on the right shoulder – a gesture not appreciated by the down to earth dalesman – 'that a lot of credit must be laid on yer wide shoulders.'

Cedric took a step back, not without some embarrassment and not sure where this unexpected praise from the unpopular bookie was leading.

'No,' continued Uneven, now getting into his stride. 'I've

been impressed by what I've seen here today and as you know Cedric' – the formality of Mr Hardcastle was soon dispensed with – 'I'm not a man without some influence and I like what I see.'

Uneven sidled a little closer to the race steward to take him into his 'confidence', a move which was not welcomed by the latter who felt his personal space invaded.

'Between you and me man, I reckon that a word in the ear of the right person and I could be looking at the next chief steward for The Plumpington Cup.'

'The Plump. . .' Cedric could hardly get the words out, so shocked was he at the revelation. His reaction was hardly surprising – the Hillthorpe and Daleswick Gala's 440 yard dog sprint and hare coursing races were one thing, but the Plumpington Cup! Named after its original patron, Lord Plumpington who owned more acres of North Yorkshire and Durham than even the King of England; that prestigious race was the highlight of the canine racing calendar in the North of England.

'No, it's true Cedric, it only takes a few words from me and you will be ordering a new set of whites for the occasion. Tell yer what, so impressed am I today, I'll even buy yer them myself when yer appointed.'

Now Cedric Hardcastle, like a true Yorkshireman, was no fool and like many a whippet and greyhound under his supervision, 'had been around the track a few times.'

'What do you want Mr Stevens?' a suspicious Cedric replied, as he took one generous step backwards from the bookmaker in the process.

'Shocked' and offended by the temerity of such a question Uneven feigned to be stunned at its undertone of suspicion.

What really hurt the disreputable Uneven was his ruse was seemingly falling on deaf ears.

'All I want, Cedric, is justice.' He turned to his associate. 'Ain't that so, Mr Nightingale?'

'Yeah, justice. . . responded a nodding Cauliflower, who at the same time moved one threatening step towards the harassed official.

'Justice, what do yer mean?' said a bemused but increasingly uncomfortable Cedric.

'I mean the next chief steward of the Plumpington Cup isn't a man who lacks judgement; not afraid to make an unpopular decision himself, of course, to right an obvious wrong,' came the reply from Uneven.

'For example, that last race. There was no way that stupid Slipper was the winner, anybody could see that. 'E may have stopped the hare in mid tracks, so to speak, but everybody could see he didn't kill it. No, from where I was standing that Bedlington, what's his name. . .' – he pretended to give it some thought – '. . .Patch. Yeah that's it, Patch. 'E was the one who beat the pack and finished it off.

'That Slipper was even knocked over senseless by the little hare – not that the mutt seemed to have much sense in the first place.' He laughed at his own joke, before continuing, 'I've never seen such a farcical thing in all my life. Have you Mr Nightingale?'

Cauliflower shook his head, before a full five seconds later blurting out: 'Never, Mr Stevens. That Patch won fair and square.'

'There you are, Cedric. Fair and square,' concluded Uneven before his 'quarry' had time to react.

'Now it would 'ardly be fair on all those who laid a bet on

Patch would it, depriving them of their due reward? Yer can see my dilemma, can't yer Cedric, being, like yerself, a fair and sportin' man?'

'Even though it will hit me in the pocket all I want to see is justice. Yer get my drift, Cedric.'

Cedric certainly did see his 'drift' and did not like the way this 'conversation' was going, and his face betrayed his feelings as it flushed red with blood, something not unnoticed by the wily bookkeeper.

'Of course, to reverse your original decision of the last race,' continued Uneven before Cedric could say anything, 'would take considerable courage on your part, but you could argue that in the interests of fair play it has to be done.

'Now the rules state categorically that the winning dog is the one who captures and kills the hare; and rules, as they say. . . is rules. And yer can't break the rules, can yer Cedric?' added the sly bookie.

Again he patted him condescendingly on the shoulder.

'I'm sure a sportin' steward of your reputation and experience will be able to convince the punters,' he hesitated, before adding, '. . . er, sporting men, that a little error has been made.

'Naturally, a respectable man like yourself should be rewarded for making such a fine, upstanding judgement. So to compensate for the understandable error of judgement on this unfortunate occasion. . .' – Uneven smiled at his own turn of phrase – '. . . apart from the certainty of you starting the Plumpington Cup, I think a more immediate reward is warranted on this occasion.'

Uneven snapped his fingers and Cauliflower dutifully offered up the Gladstone bag he had been preciously guarding and opened it before Cedric.

The bookmaker took out four white banknotes and proffered them to the stunned race steward.

'It's what I call the price of justice,' smirked Uneven, thrusting the folded notes into the top pocket of Cedric's not so white and faded coat.

However, the usual compliant reaction to this manoeuvre by the bookie was not forthcoming on this occasion.

Seeing the chief steward's reaction he quickly added. 'Of course, that money would go to a charity of your, er, choice.'

Immediately Cedric took out the paper money notes stuffed in his pocket and threw them back at Uneven in pure disgust.

'Who the 'ell do yer think yer are, lad?' bellowed an indignant Cedric. 'You can't buy me with yer dirty money. I'm not lyin' or cheatin' for anybody, let alone a low life like you.

'If yer want to repeat what yer just said to me in front of witnesses – not that yer gorilla here counts as a witness – please go ahead.'

The gorilla was not pleased with this remark and grunted.

'As far as I'm concerned,' added the steward, 'that Slipper won the race fair and square and nothin' yer can say or 'ow many dirty bribes yer offer will change that fact,' declared a clearly furious Cedric.

'Now take your money and get off my course before I call the police,' he warned.

Being called a cheat, a low life and someone who offers bribes was just water off a duck's back to Uneven Stephens – he could take that; but what he could not abide was his reputation as a 'fixer' being questioned in the racing community, and that his attempts to bend an official had not even got out of the traps.

The head bookie and his 'gorilla' where not happy men and even Uneven could not control his temper, and all his bottled venom came pouring out like lava bursting from a volcano.

He grabbed hold of Cedric by both his lapels and threateningly shoved his face directly into that of the plucky race steward, so they were nose to nose before he hissed: 'Yer announce a steward's inquiry or we'll break yer bleedin' legs. Is that straight enuff for yer? Do it or yer be in Maltby Hospital before the next race,' sneered the bookie with menace.

Cedric's face went whiter than his coat. Cauliflower licked his lips at a bit of 'action' but before Cedric could gasp out another word Da, Arthur and Tommy, accompanied by Patch and Slipper, came on the scene – not liking what they appeared to be seeing from across the field.

'What's up, Cedric?' asked Da, clearly not convinced this was an amicable 'conversation' between the bookie, his henchman, and the race steward.

Bravely Cedric told the truth.

''Ee's been threatening me Joe. Tried to bribe me too,' stammered a clearly shaken Cedric. 'Wanted me to say your Patch won the race, claiming that Slipper hadn't made the kill.'

''Ee what!' fumed Da, clearly affronted but not entirely shocked by what he was hearing.

'Did he tell yer Cedric, that Uneven had taken a bet of £10 off Arthur 'ere at odds of 20-1. When Slipper won he lost £200.'

'The cheatin'. . .' exclaimed an irate Arthur, but before he could say anything else, Uneven – who had rapidly calculated the odds if things turned 'physical' – suddenly regained his composure.

'Now, now then lads,' he said, with as much bonhomie as he could muster, 'I think there's been a slight misunderstanding 'ere and Cedric has got hold of the wrong end of the stick.'

'I don't think so,' said Da, clearly not impressed with the weaselly bookie.

'All I'm saying is that Slipper didn't make the kill. Everyone could see that,' argued Uneven, 'it just makes the race null and void, that's all, and in the circumstances all bets are off!'

'Why you,' Da had to quickly restrain Arthur who was ready to take a swing at the unethical Uneven.

Cauliflower stepped forward ready to punch the next man, or boy, to move.

'Now, come lads, you know I'm a fair man,' was the final appeal by the bookie to turn the situation to his favour.

'Technically it was true. Uneven Stephens was a fair man; his background was in the travelling fairs where his family, for centuries, if they were not in gaol, roamed across the north and east of England, stealing, mugging, extracting extortion money and rigging prize fights – a bad apple, who gave the majority of the Romany race an undeserved poor reputation.

'I suggest,' said Da, with all the authority he could muster, 'that you pay Arthur what e's owed and what is rightfully his and call it a day.'

'Or else what,' sneered Uneven, not willing to back down. Cauliflower 'unveiled' a cosh from inside his jacket to accentuate his boss's point. Da coughed nervously, as he knew he had got himself into dangerous waters but knew he could not now back down.

Tommy was worried for his father, who was a sick man and would be at a severe disadvantage if it came to any violence.

Things turned even nastier when two more paid thugs, summoned by a signal from the bookie, barged into the proceedings from behind Da and Arthur, and added their 'weight' to the dispute. One of them Tommy recognised as Archie Tilsley's dad, with whom there was already 'bad blood' between him and his Da when they worked together down the mine.

Arthur, Da and even Tommy knew that when it came to a 'scrap' they were both at a disadvantage physically and numerically – a fact not lost on Uneven, who with a wicked leer on his face, dared them to throw the first punch.

But the second miracle of the day happened that moment, one that would be talked about in legendary terms for years in the snug of the Colliers' Arms as 'the Battle of Ramsden's Field'.

When Cauliflower looked to be taking out his cosh, Patch feared for his Master and Young Master and only his quick actions saved the day.

The terrier, angered by the cowardly and belligerent bookie and his thugs, let out a throaty howl – a howl with the scale of his biggest Bedlington Roar, which pierced the air and could be heard far beyond the showground.

His plaintive and primeval cry was joined by Slipper, who although he was not sure what it was for, joined in anyway for the fun of it – helping to double its resonance.

Their unexpected howling did not stop Uneven, who was losing his temper and eager for 'action', taking the first swing at Da; fortunately Da ducked and the bookie's fist missed its target. Even more narked at this latest humiliation Uneven was now ready to do serious damage – as was Cauliflower who raised his heavy cosh ready to batter any unfortunate who got in his way – friend or foe!

Things looked bad for Da and his brave little 'gang', who had refused to back down against the intimidating band of thugs. At that moment, if there developed any scrap, there was only one dead cert as to the winner.

When all looked lost, a sight never before, nor since, was seen fast approaching on the field from below the brow of the hillock. In response to Patch's 'war cry' 24 dogs of all assorted breeds – and non breeds – were pulling at the leashes attached to their owners who were members of the Hillthorpe and Daleswick Dog Owners' Association.

It was a vision that Da, Arthur, Tommy and Cedric would remember for the rest of their lives.

'It's the bloomin' cavalry,' grinned Tommy, who partial to the odd western himself on a Saturday afternoon at the church hall, enjoyed a Tom Mix cowboy film at the 'flicks'.

When word got round that 'sleazebag' Stevens and his henchmen were threatening their chief steward, the landlord of their beloved pub the Colliers' Arms, along with a hardworking and respected miner and his bairn, then it was their fight too!

On two and four legs the 'posse' thrust forward as one, with determination to go into battle.

The 'battle' ensued as Uneven took another lunge at Da, this time with a glancing blow. Da rocked unsteadily on his feet but stood his ground. Tommy waded in to protect his dad and kicked the bookie hard in the shins; it was a good job he was wearing his steel capped boot that day! Uneven let out a cry of pain just as Cauliflower was about to lift his cosh to whip Tommy with a potentially fatal blow. Patch, alert to the danger, sprang at him and gripped the 'gorilla's hand' for all he was worth, forcing the 'associate' to release his grip of the weapon, which fell on the floor. Patch, now in a frenzy, that only a Bedlington could understand, then turned on the main perpetrator of the mêlée and sank his teeth hard into the rear end of Uneven, who was still recovering and in pain from a near broken shin.

Slipper, who did not really comprehend quite what was happening and thought it all a great game, copied his pal and sank his teeth into the conveniently placed but unfortunate Cedric Hardcastle. Fortunately for the chief steward, the whippet's bite was as soft as his head and he didn't feel a thing.

Da, although he should not have been fighting in his state of health, took one almighty swing and landed a beauty on Tilsley's nose – the villain squealed with pain; Da had never felt such satisfaction in his life – apart, of course, from when he married Ma and the birth of his four children!

After Patch finally released his grip on Uneven, the bookmaker looked up and saw the advancing cavalry and realised it was time to 'hedge his bets' and make a retreat. Cauliflower too was in trouble; after having his hand badly mauled Tommy decided that the thug deserved a kick in the shins as well and soon the villainous gang were seen frantically running, or hobbling, for sanctuary over the nearest field wall, pursued by the snarling and barking pack of racing dogs and their owners.

Da turned to his 'heroic band of brothers' and proclaimed: 'Eh lads, I think Napoleon has just met his Waterloo!' and a loud cheer went up across the 'battlefield' along with a few howls and barks of approval from the canine fraternity. The Battle of Ramsden's Field was won!

However, there was more elation to come. The spoils of victory included a Gladstone bag stuffed full of banknotes, guineas and silver coin – the day's total of Uneven Stevens mostly illegal earnings were, surprisingly, abandoned by the villains but retrieved by the observant Patch, who dropped the bag in front of his Young Master.

Tommy, after gleefully patting Patch on his tuft in recognition, dutifully gave the cash laden bag to his Da. Da took out £200 and gave it to a beaming Arthur, who was grinning from ear to ear.

'I swear to you Joe, and to all yer members of the Hillthorpe and Daleswick Dog Racing Owners' Association, I will never make another bet as long as I live.'

In true Yorkshire style, Da proclaimed to Arthur: 'Eh lad, I think the first round is on thee tonight at the Colliers' for the next meeting of the dog owners and friends!' With that Da heartily slapped his pal on the back, a gesture welcomed once again with delight by his landlord friend.

'Neh lad, make it the first two rounds,' laughed Arthur holding out his newly acquired wealth.

But the humiliation, a sore backside and shin, the loss of his day's illegal earnings and the ruination of his reputation was not the only loss for Uneven Stevens that day. For it was Skipper, who while sniffing around the field of battle brought back an even greater trophy to the assembled sporting men – bigger to them than the Plumpington Cup itself. For as he lay at his master's feet, the ever hungry Slipper, sunk his teeth into the pages of a certain little black book that contained all the illegal bets accepted and monies owed to one of the district's most despised characters.

Everybody laughed and Patch wagged his tail in knowing delight as Slipper looked perplexed at all this sudden attention.

After Arthur had paid for the first two rounds he decided to return the money to the community 'pot'; and that was how, thanks to a 'mysterious' benefactor, a substantial contribution found its way to Hillthorpe Chapel and the members of the Hillthorpe and Daleswick Racing Dog Owners' Association, and all were sporting new white overalls at the next race. Oh, and all the doggy members each were given half a dozen of Fishwick's finest sausages.

Many a tail wagged that night and some even belonged to the doggy members of the village.

15

Catastrophe at the Cat Show

NOW the Hillthorpe and Daleswick Miners' Annual Gala Day may well have been 'the big un' on the North Yorkshire community's social calendar, but for the canines and felines of the district and their owners there was only one event which was the cat's whiskers (or top dog) of the year. That was the Hillthorpe and Daleswick Dog and Cat Show.

Not the 'Hillthorpe and Daleswick Cat and Dog Show' it must be noted, which ruffled the fur of the feline folk, who quite reasonably argued that the letter 'C' was before the letter 'D' in the alphabet – the order of the show title had been established in Queen Victoria's golden jubilee year by the original show secretary and chairman Albert Hoggins, a local farmer and owner of two outstanding border collies, Nip and Tuck. It was hardly surprising to most people that Nip came out champion dog in the inaugural year, with Tuck as reserve – there was just a whisker between them.

It was claimed by a few wagging tails and tongues that if Albert Hoggins had had his way entirely, Tuck would have been named 'best cat in show' to compensate for being runner up in the canine crown! A catty remark but the precedent was set on the judging standards and such criticism was 'par for the course' in the local dog and cat show world, where a 'you scratch my back and I'll scratch yours' was the norm amongst owners, judges and, sadly, even many of the cat contestants themselves.

There was, of course, the infamous scandal of 1911 at the Dog and Cat Show, when Nobby Norton, a 'newcomer' to Daleswick (Nobby was from a mining family that had moved to the village in 1823 from Hemsley, 12 miles away, seeking employment), saw his pet win 'best cat in show', even though it had half an ear missing due to its prowess as a rat catcher – its left earlobe being removed after taking on two rodents one winter's evening and 'biting off more than it could chew' – which also could be said for one of his opponents that day.

No, it was proven that Nobby had 'nobbled' one of the cat judges, a certain Sefton Riley, with a sizeable bribe, the transaction of which was witnessed one beery night in the Colliers' Arms.

The 'unimpeachable' defence by Mr Riley of 'I didn't take Mr Norton's £5 (nobody up to that point had mentioned it was £5, not even the witness) was made substantially worse for the accused when he added: 'Besides, what's wrong with selling a title or two – if it's good enough for Lloyd George and his Government, it's good enough for the Dales.'

The plea did not endear Mr Riley to the Hillthorpe and Daleswick Dog and Cat Show standards' committee and he was forced to resign on the spot, having committed the crime of being caught – which no disrespecting, bent judge would ever have done in the first place.

Of course, in this 'cat and dog' environment there was usually one owner that managed to claw her way to the top in the annual competition, proving Darwinian evolutionary theory, and that was the formidable figure of Prudence Popplethwaite. When it came to the cat show jungle, Mrs P was its lioness – ready to pounce on any 'contender' to her throne and skin them alive.

It was not the rewards on offer that attracted such a large number of competitors each year to the annual cat and dog shows – the top prize ran to a ten shilling voucher from Mr Hardwick's Ironmongery and two dozen beef sausages from Fishwick's (a prize not unnoticed by a certain Bedlington terrier from Hillthorpe). No, the main reason for its popularity was that in a small but proud community such competitions offered a certain amount of prestige to the 'victor' and a reflection of their status in the two mining villages – especially to such folk as Prudence Popplethwaite, who liked nothing more than to 'get one over' on her neighbours.

For the past five years the 'Empress of India' trophy – as donated by the late Colonel Wellesley-Smythe, a former colonial officer of the Raj and past commander-in-chief of the King's Own North Yorkshire Volunteers – went to the best cat in show. It was a splendid trophy, adorned with a silver leaping tiger, on a plated base with the names of former winners engraved – the names of the pet owners but not the cats themselves.

The trophy stood, with pride of place, in the front bay window of Mrs Popplethwaite's home – a public position to not only remind any passer-by (if indeed they needed to be reminded) of Mrs P's prowess and achievements as a cat owner but also, not that she would admit it, as a 'warning' or a gauntlet thrown down to any possible usurper of her title.

Her previous cat Fang, a pedigree Siamese, which was the unfortunate holder of its mistress's affections, had won the cat show titles in 1909 and 1910.

Mrs Popplethwaite, chairwoman of the Hillthorpe and Daleswick Cat Show committee, was a formidable lady, and not one to confront in 'open combat' if it could be avoided – a bit like the local rodent population when taking on her present feline, Genghis.

So thus when Fang, as expected (expected in the sense of whom his owner happened to be), won the Empress of India trophy for the second time unexpectedly (unexpectedly because, despite, or because of, its owner the pampered cat was by far the worst behaved animal entrant at the show that year) – foul play was suspected.

Of course, nothing could be proven but, when in the final judging, the other cats in contention, who before then were cute and placid creatures and fine examples of the feline species, suddenly began to miaow and jump dementedly about like 'cats on a hot tin roof', it all seemed very 'fishy'.

A mysterious white powder was found on all the finalists' cat paws, all except those belonging to Fang. However, despite what appeared damning evidence the judges had no choice but to award 'the best in show' to Fang, for, in the circumstances, his 'good behaviour'. Their confidence in the newly crowned cat must have been undermined when Fang scratched the unfortunate judge, Reverend Segdwick, when he had the temerity (or stupidity) to give the winner a friendly pat on the head. By then it was too late to rescind the prize and a timely glare by Mrs Popplethwaite herself at the cowed reverend was enough to conclude the ceremony.

Although a tin of bicarbonate soda was spotted by a fellow cat owner when Mrs P opened her enormous handbag at the customary refreshments among the cat owners after the prize giving, it was too late.

'Besides,' proclaimed the formidable and unperturbed Mrs Popplethwaite, 'I take this bicarbonate for a medical condition. I was told by Doctor Crippler, my personal physician, to take it twice a day. It is scientifically proven to reduce flatulence.'

This statement, to those in range of Mrs P's booming voice, certainly took the wind out of any possible accuser's sails.

In less than thirty minutes of regaining the title for a second time Mrs P paraded the Empress of India trophy, once again, as it appeared defiantly in the bay window of a certain household.

Now, as laid down by the rules of the cat competition (or in truth, belatedly at the last committee meeting, as urged by the chairwoman herself), it was declared that if any winner of the cat trophy won it three times in a row, the Empress of India could be kept by the 'fortunate' owner. A new, replica trophy would be sought and replaced under the terms of Colonel Willoughby-Smythe's will.

Unfortunately for Mrs Popplethwaite, as she was making preparations well in advance of the competition to defend the title and claim the trophy out right, Fang passed to the cattery in the sky.

The official version is that Fang, on a rare escape from its owner's clutches, fell down a well. The next day, the parish council, under a barrage of accusations of incompetence from Mrs P, put an iron safety grill over the 'offending' well. The fact that a child could have easily fallen in and befallen the same fate as Fang was her winning argument that caused the authorities to act immediately.

No one was certain exactly how the mishap had happened, but the conclusion was, by many, that the thuggish Fang had fallen down the 'unsecured' well. Another theory, though, spoken out of earshot of Mrs P, and one more popular in the two villages, was that the unfortunate Fang had committed 'caticide' and thrown itself in – stressed out by the double unfortunate demands on its shoulders of living with its capricious owner combined with the expectations of an unprecedented third, successive, trophy win at the Hillthorpe and Daleswick Dog and Cat Show.

Unfortunately for the Hillthorpe animal populous, Mrs Popplethwaite, the day after the mysterious death of Fang, acquired a replacement for her affections; in her own words 'to help deaden her grief' – this time in the shape of a Mongolian cross misfit she called Genghis. It was a fact that Mrs P had 'bought' the kitten from a travelling circus which had been performing in nearby Maltby. The lion tamer whom it belonged to was more than happy to rid himself of the spiteful, uncontrollable creature; such was his eagerness he even 'threw in' a basket to cart the 'pet' away.

However, local legend had it that Genghis did not come from the circus but mysteriously 'appeared' one night when Mrs Popplethwaite and members of her coven were out dancing one moonlit night naked on the nearby moors – this was the version that the Wagstaff children and the rest of the village eagerly believed.

If ever an owner and a cat were suitably as one in both physicality and spirit it was the malevolent moggy Genghis and his mean, meddling mistress. Indeed, if there was one sole aim in Mrs P's 'raison d'etre' then it was to be the owner of the title 'Supreme champion cat of the Hillthorpe and Daleswick Dog and Cat Show' – an honour that Genghis himself not only assumed was his by divine right but, like his owner, he was prepared to do anything to make sure 'justice' was his.

In 1911, Genghis's first year as an entrant, Mrs Popplethwaite had already completed her 'spade work' to smooth her cat's path to the crown. This was suitably achieved by coming to 'an understanding' with the chairman of judges, Edwin Bagshaw – if he expected his cauliflowers to retain top prize in the horticultural section at the annual gala (bearing in mind that Mrs P herself was that year's chairman of this particular competition), then surely such a majestic specimen as Genghis was destined for 'top cat'. Subtlety was not Prudence Popplethwaite's forte.

However, that year Genghis had already played his part in his mistresses' Machiavellian machinations. Two nights before the show, on his evening 'stroll' around Hillthorpe, Genghis had paid a 'visit' to two of his likely contenders. At the back of the Colliers' Arms, in the cellar, the tomcat had taken by surprise and cornered a tremulous Tipples, between a wall and a barrel of best bitter, and stuck its claws into the good natured cat – drawing blood and inflicting two nasty wounds on each of Tipples' haunches, which, as intended, was not only painful for the poor pub pussy but highly visible to the judges. Tipples let out an almighty scream, which the whole pub could hear, and alerted the little she cat's canine friend Slipper, who galloped boldly to the rescue. The gallant whippet was sharp enough to arrive on the scene of the crime and see the assailant hastily making its way through the open back door of the cellar. Slipper gave chase and, although no animal in Hillthorpe or the surrounding district was faster in a fair race, the crafty Mongolian menace jumped and sprang up to the top of a wall, scampering along its edge and down via a nearby shed roof to shrug off his pursuer. Frustrated by the assailant's getaway the worried whippet had no choice but to give up the chase and return to the cellar to console his friend, the victim.

The incident was related by Slipper to his pal Patch at a pub 'bow-wow' later that evening.

Mission accomplished and uplifted by his recent malevolent success, 'the Evil One' targeted another likely show 'rival' – Socks, the tomcat who belonged to the Stefferson family. This time no violence was necessary, especially after word soon got around about the pub incident; a simple hostile miaow by Genghis in the right ear of a shaken Socks was enough to do the trick. In fact, at the show's final, the mere presence of the Mongolian menace, combined with a malicious stare, so unsettled the sensitive Socks that it became a quivering wreck and was soon ruled out by the judges.

That year was Genghis's first taste of victory as supreme champion and similar tactics employed by the cat and its owner ensured further success again in 1912.

Therefore, at the Hillthorpe and Daleswick Dog and Cat Show of 1913 history was set to be in the making – with Genghis firm favourite to take that unprecedented third consecutive crown and Mrs Popplethwaite to wrap her plump, stubby fingers, and keep in perpetuity, the elegant Empress of India trophy.

However, not everything was going to Mrs P's machiavellian plan. Each year the cat show had difficulty, not surprisingly, in finding suitable judges and particularly that of chief arbiter. Much to Mrs P's irritation and comprehension, she herself could not be either chief judge, or even a 'mere' judge of the cat show, as well as an owner entrant. Despite her best attempts to have 'this ridiculous rule' changed in committee, it was one that the normally compliant show's standards' committee stood firm on. It was also the reason why Mrs P had to 'make do' with lesser posts at the show, such as chairman of the horticultural section, in order for her to continue pulling the levers of her considerable influence at the event.

However, undeterred, the resilient and resolute Mrs Popplethwaite, pressed ahead with her scheme to capture the ultimate prize – one which was now surely in her grasp. Her hopes were raised when her 'ally' and near social equal – Mrs Curtois-Pughs – was, backed by Mrs P herself, elevated to cat show chairman. This was a masterly (or mistressly) coup for Mrs Popplethwaite – the 'understanding' between the two tabbies was for Genghis to secure the cat crown and Mrs C-P's dog, the annoyingly pampered pooch Archie, to be 'anointed' supreme champion dog.

So everything was set for the cat show final – out of a healthy entry of 33 cats from the Hillthorpe and Daleswick district, the three judges had selected their final six.

Genghis, as reigning and twice champion 'naturally' took his place among the elite. Socks, whose previous encounter with last year's victor meant he steadfastly dug his claws in and refused to enter as soon as he was taken by Freda Stefferson towards the village hall – miaowing like a cat possessed and leaping from the girl's arms before running away towards the sanctuary of his home. However, suspecting that Socks would act in this way, the Steffersons brought along in reserve their other feline, Flossie – a likeable, timid little creature, who was totally oblivious of the occasion and content to curl up on the top of the judging table where the contestants were paraded and have her usual afternoon 'cat nap'.

Then there was Tipples, who a year older, brazenly refused to be bullied into withdrawing from the competition, and although scarred for life by the previous assault – though, now, with the deep scratches healed and her unsightliness covered by fur – bravely resisted the 'evil eye' of Genghis to take her place in the final – no doubt supplemented with some 'Dutch courage', courtesy of a few chosen slops from the beer tray from the Colliers' Arms that lunchtime.

The other three contenders were Tinkerbell, a cute, young female whose owner, Maud Mason, had tied a little bell around its collar which used to tinkle; Ginger, who although as pretty as a picture and living up to his name in colouring, was hampered in his chances by one unfortunate habit which was shortly to be revealed. Finally there was Winston, an aristocratic cat, with impeccable ill-breeding, who was short, tubby and losing his fur, but who, like Genghis, was ambitious to reach the top and make a name for himself.

There were three judges – Ernie Wickes, the local postman, whose experience over the years with the canines of the animal kingdom made him a natural for the cat preference camp. The second, Miss Winifred Mayfield, a cat loving spinster, who lived with six felines – or more accurately, waited on her 'babies' hand and foot in 'cat castle' as her home was locally dubbed by local schoolchildren. Along with Mrs P and Mrs C-P, Miss M was undoubtedly one of the 'tabby trio' in Hillthorpe – or 'coven' as termed by those of less flattering disposition.

Then, of course, there was Mrs Curtois-Pughs herself, who 'naturally' assumed the leadership of the judging panel as befitted her social standing and self-proclaimed abilities. She was certainly dressed to impress, having bought a new outfit especially for the occasion, topped off with a hat that would have graced Royal Ascot and a long, exotic, feather boa draped around her neck – an item never seen before in the mining community.

There was quite a crowd packed in Hillthorpe Church Hall that day, as there always was for the annual cat show; however, those who gathered were not only there to enjoy a fine collection of moggies but also other show attractions – the competitions for best rabbit and best goldfish being of particular interest to the children of the two villages.

Among those looking forward to the event were Ma Wagstaff, who had come along with little Emma and Tommy accompanied by Patch, who was noted by many, incuding Miss Mayfield herself, 'such a well behaved young dog, a fine example of his species, particularly when surrounded by so many cats.'

'If only others dogs could behave, in such an impeccable way,' she remarked to Ma.

Patch wagged his tail in appreciation of this gracious remark.

As usual there was a vibrant atmosphere amid contestants, creatures and their supporters, as judges of the three categories passed up and down the tables, examining, prodding, poking and staring at the fine specimens before them – before pontificating among themselves and discussing the merits of each cat, rabbit and goldfish that had entered.

After much deliberation the three judges were ready to reveal their revered decisions to the expectant crowd – the atmosphere now akin to what it must be for the masses gathered on St Peter's Square in Rome, waiting for white smoke to belch out of a Vatican chimney to signal the election of a new pope.

Ernie Wickes cleared his throat and banged one of the tables with a wooden mallet to demand silence, before introducing Mrs Curtois-Pughs to announce the results. The vibration, though, and sudden loud banging, frightened poor Flossie, who was still half asleep from her afternoon siesta, and she bolted through the door in the same direction as her 'brother' Socks had earlier.

Genghis let out a low purr of satisfaction, knowing the odds of his victory had just been reduced from 6 to 1 to 5 to 1 – not that the result in his mind was in doubt. These odds were further reduced to 4 to 1, when Ginger, surely one of the crowd favourites, chose that very moment to spit up a huge fur ball, before generating a small pool of vomit right in front of the judges.

'After an extremely difficult decision,' droned Mrs Curtois-Pughs, 'and much deliberation from my esteemed panel of judges,' without showing any sign of humility, she continued unabated. . . 'I. . .' she gave a little cough, correcting herself. . . 'I mean, we, have great pleasure in announcing the champion rabbit of the Hillthorpe and

Daleswick pet show for 1913 is. . .' She allowed time for dramatic pause and to focus maximum attention on her good self. . . 'is. . .' another dramatic pause. . . 'Hoppy.'

There was a squeal of delight from its proud owner eight year-old Daisy Dewhurst and a polite round of applause from the other owners as well as the appreciative crowd.

With much further ado, and an equal measure of pomposity, Mrs Curtois-Pughs then proceeded to put the entrants of the goldfish competition out of their misery.

. . .'And the winner is, after much consultation, and may I congratulate the quality of this year's entrants, the winner is. . . (more dramatic pause). . . Moby.'

Moby's owner, ten year-old Bertie Robinson, was so delighted that he looked fit to burst his gills. Again, there was more polite and friendly applause for this popular victory.

Now just before the announcement that everybody had been waiting for – that of who was going to take the title of supreme champion cat – Patch decided to take matters into his own paws.

As was the custom of the prize winning ceremony, in the middle of the top table was placed the resplendent Empress of India trophy; the judges then placed next to it the top rabbit, Hoppy, along with the jam jar almost filled with water, containing the top goldfish, Moby, to be admired by all.

This table was flanked on its left by the top six cat entries, with Genghis, naturally, positioned the nearest one next to the trophy for convenience of prize giving, as requested by Mrs Curtois-Pughs – while on the right were the other top entries of the rabbit and goldfish competitions.

Conveniently for Patch, Mrs C-P made the most of building up the suspense to reveal the name of the cat show champion, doing her best to hold everyone's attention; it gave the little dog chance to make his move.

For the previous thirty minutes Patch had been obediently at the heels of Mistress Ma, Young Master Tommy and little Emma, who themselves had come to witness the popular village spectacle. So well behaved was the Bedlington that none of the Wagstaffs had noticed his brief disappearance from their sides. For while everyone's attention was on the chief judge and which cat would be named the champion of the year, the terrier made his way, covertly, under the draped covers of the top table.

With the judges' decision about to be made, Mrs Popplethwaite scrambled for position nearer the top table in expectation of her magical moment; she swept past the owners of Tinkerbell and Ginger, and with flailing elbows pushed past little Albert Dobbins, the young owner of finalist Winston, and stood right in front of him so she could be nearest to Mrs C-P for 'presentation purposes'.

Patch, unnoticed behind the drapes of the tablecloth, looked to see the stubby tail of Genghis invitingly dangling, unknowingly by its owner, and flicking in front of the terrier's face. On another day this would have been a most satisfying target but clamping his jaws around Genghis's tail, as he did with such great effect on that unforgettable animal service at the chapel, was not in Patch's plans this day. No, he had other 'fish to fry'.

For fortuitously, just out of paw's reach by Genghis, across the adjoining table, sat the jam jar containing Hillthorpe's and Daleswick's new champion goldfish, Moby.

Patch, seizing this surely heaven sent opportunity from the Great Bedlington in the Sky, took between his jaws the bottom nap of the tablecloth; the subtle effect was that the jar and Moby became mobile – both glass container and its occupant slid very slowly four inches nearer the adjoining table. Nobody, accept Patch and Moby, noticed this slight change of position, although Genghis, preening himself in preparation for his inevitable 'enthronement' gave a slight, sly glance to his left before returning his regal gaze to the chief judge, Mrs Curtois-Pughs.

'Now I am sure that you are all waiting most expectantly for the name of the winning cat in this year's show and without further ado. . . she paused, dramatically and made quite an ado in looking around at all in the crowd to make sure she had everyone under her spell.

'Oh,' she continued, 'I must say before I announce the winner. . .' she looked around the crowd before fixing her gaze and giving a 'gracious' nod to her 'ally', Mrs Popplethwaite who, with a smile that any self-respecting Cheshire cat would have been proud of, was almost purring herself in satisfaction.

'This competition, I must say to all the cat owners present, has been the closest and most difficult to judge for many a year. 'I. . . ' she coughed slightly again before making a slight, self-conscious adjustment. . . 'We, the judges, have never seen such standards achieved before.'

'Get on with it you old windbag,' piped up Bert Dyson, before his dad, standing behind him, gave him a cuff around the ear, albeit with a grin on his face, while the rest of the assembled tittered in agreement.

Mrs Curtois-Pughs ignored this 'uncouth' interruption.

. . .'The supreme champion cat of the Hillthorpe and Daleswick Dog and Cat show 1913 is. . . (another dramatic pause). . .

Mrs Popplethwaite looked adoringly at her beloved Genghis, her ample bosom swelling with pride at what was to be her finest moment, when her 'baby' was to be crowned three times champion and attain for her the sole ownership of the coveted trophy – the Empress of India silver cup. Her stays were almost bursting with pride.

It was at that very point that Patch gave a final dainty tug at the trailing table drape and Moby and jam jar were once again on the move.

Genghis, who was taking great pleasure in seeing his personal servant, Mrs Popplethwaite, beaming with pride at his impending achievement; his heart (yes, contrary to popular rumour among the Hillthorpe animal kingdom, the district's most unpopular feline did possess one – in physical form, if not one of the compassionate variety) beat, at that moment, in true syncopation with that of his so-called mistress a few feet away.

For Genghis, who up to that moment had, by his impeccably low standards, acted with all the majestic bearing of one who surely knew 'his time for greatness was about to be thrust upon him', stretched his neck and looked up towards the heavens – anticipating the forthcoming moment of his anointment and glory.

Well, unexpectedly, it would certainly be a moment he would never forget in his nine lives and an incident that would be talked about for years, never to be forgotten, by those privileged to be present at the prize giving ceremony that day.

. . . 'The winner is Gen. . . '

Unfortunately, at that critical point for the 'impending champion' and his mistress/servant, there could not have been a worse time for the Mongolian monster to respond to his primeval instincts.

Mrs Curtois-Pughs, with the Empress of India trophy firmly in hand, took a step towards a beaming Mrs Popplethwaite but was confronted by a sight of horror that froze her both in movement and speech.

For just in his moment of supreme triumph, as the figure of Mrs Curtois-Pughs flounced before him and was beginning to mouth his name to proclaim him champion, Genghis saw, out the corner of his ever alert eye, the glistening, shimmering form of Moby – who now, thanks to Patch's efforts, was within the cat's paw's reach. With all the speed and accuracy of a great athlete and the eye to paw co-ordination that any member of his species would have been proud of, within the bat of a bat's eyelid, the Mongolian monster flicked out his left paw, inserted it into the jar, pulled out the unsuspecting Moby in one fluent motion, before thrusting the little, wiggling goldfish down his greedy gullet. The prey had been reeled in – hook, line and goldfish!

Poor Moby – just like from one of Patch's favourite Mistress Ma's stories – must have felt like Jonah being swallowed whole by the whale but unlike the Biblical story, there was no 'happy ending' with the 'hero' being spat out alive and in one piece.

No, instead, in this sorry saga, Genghis swallowed ravenously, licking his lips in sublime satisfaction before, true to form, adding the crime of atrocious bad manners to his heinous behaviour by loudly emitting a contented belch.

His actions brought a gasp of collective horror from a stunned and equally revolted crowd. This first wave of sound from the shock was soon replaced by the wail of a distraught little Bertie Robinson, the former owner of the aforementioned goldfish Moby, who now to everybody's embarrassment and sympathy, burst into a flood of tears.

Patch, his work now complete, tip-pawed his way back from under the top table, making sure that that he was unobserved and not touching anyone's legs, before resuming his sitting 'obedient' position at the side of his mistress. He snuggled his nose into her dress to quickly draw her attention. Despite her shock at the public spectacle she had just witnessed of the 'Mongolian Murderer' Ma looked at the beseeching, doleful, innocent eyes of her loyal Patch and reached down with her hand to pat the top of his head.

'Good boy, Patch,' she smiled adoringly at the little dog beside her, 'good job I haven't got a nasty, vicious brute of an animal for a pet.'

Patch felt a warm shiver from the welcome acknowledgement of his presence by his beloved mistress – added to which his alibi was now in place!

As Bertie's parents tried to console their inconsolable son, a wave of outrage surfaced from the crowd.

'Savage beast', 'absolute disgrace', 'monster' and 'nasty, vicious brute', were some of the more gracious remarks piercing the air.

'That cursed cat ought to be put down,' expressed one irate villager who had previous experience of the 'accused' when her cat, Tiger – who had unfortunately not lived up to his chosen name – had come off worse a few weeks earlier after a ferocious spat with Genghis in a Hillthorpe back alley.

A clearly ruffled Mrs Popplethwaite was seeing her year of persuasion, planning and plotting unravel before her eyes – like the ball of wool she once foolishly left in the same room as her cat, that was soon in a state of no use to either woman or intended tea cosy.

However, admirably, Mrs P tried to defend the indefensible.

'My Genghis is a cat,' she blurted out – it was hard to argue with the opening statement – before adding to anyone who would listen, 'he was only following his instincts!'

It was a plausible defence but these words were not enough to abate the surge of anger by the majority of those in the hall – man, woman, child, and indeed beast. It certainly could not dam the tears flowing from the cheeks, nor the wails of despair, from Master Robinson.

While the humans expressed their displeasure in vocal form all the other animals in the room made their disgust known by turning their backs on 'the despised and guilty Genghis' – even the goldfish mouthed silently their resentment in language only known to fellow pisceans.

Any words of mitigation on behalf of the 'Evil One' were lost on a crowd whose sympathies lay with little Bertie Robinson and the recently departed Moby. Indeed, poor Bertie had cried enough tears to refill the empty, glass jar that lay, like exhibit A, innocuously on its side on the water stained table.

However, the unfortunate catastrophe – or 'goldfishtrophe' would be a better choice if that word was ever included in the English dictionary – could not hide the fact that a new supreme champion cat of the Hillthorpe and Daleswick Dog and Cat Show had now to be named.

Mrs Curtois-Pughs, whose haughtiness knew no bounds and usually brushed aside any criticism, could not help but sense the strength of repulsion by those in the room for the two 'cats' in front of her – one of which was Genghis. She now had a 'difficult and swift choice' to make – to do the 'honourable' thing – stand by her friend and carry out their 'pact' by anointing Mrs Popplethwaite's pet as show champion – or the 'dishonourable' but easier thing and succumb to overwhelming public sentiment and cave in to the voice of the mob. To a woman of her temperament and backbone in the face of adversity it was an obvious choice.

She instructed her 'fellow judge' Ernie Wickes to demand order. The moment was enjoyed by the latter, who again had the chance to wield his gavel and bang hard on the wooden table to demand attention – and by doing so, just adding more consternation to the animals and fish present.

'Order, order,' he barked, as if in His Majesty's Crown Court and all eyes turned once again to the chief judge, Mrs Curtois-Pughs.

Sheepishly and trying not to look anyone in the eye, and a certain lady in particular, she – clearly embarrassed by the turn of events and wanting, desperately, to get the whole thing over – proclaimed to the assembled:

'The supreme champion cat for the Hillthorpe and Daleswick Dog and Cat Show 1913 is. . . (there was no dramatic pause). . . Tipples.'

A great cheer went up in the crowd. There was no doubting it was a very popular choice, except for one lady bedecked in a floral print match with ill-matching hat and accessories. Another cheer went up when Flossie was named reserve champion, to the delight of Freda Stefferson.

Prudence Popplethwaite, though, let out an exasperated gasp of indignation at such 'injustice'.

Her first thought was that the weekly 'stitch and bitch' meetings with that 'traitor' Curtois-Pughs were cancelled forthwith.

As for the new supreme champion, Tipples, the amenable pub cat could not believe her luck at having such an honour bestowed and gave a purr of satisfaction, before deciding it was all too much and proceeding to curl up on the table, ignore all the fuss around her and close her eyes for another snooze. Besides, reasoned Tipples, surely there would be more celebrations at the Colliers' Arms later that evening to look forward to and the odd 'tipple' from a clearly elated and proud Mrs Tankard, her owner.

If ever there was an award for the most outraged cat in the world that moment then surely it must have gone to Genghis. He hissed and spat and hissed again and would have drawn blood if his sharp claws were not just out of swipe range from Mrs Curtois-Pughs, who was a particular target of his venom.

All his pent-up frustration at this indignity in front of all the village had to have its outlet and Genghis, not one to hold in his emotions, jumped and scampered all over the hall in a demented frenzy – knocking off the table and smashing two fishbowls to the floor to add two more murders to his lengthy criminal record before leaping for the throat at Mrs C-P with claws outstretched. Luckily the shocked chief judge was saved from the venom of Genghis by a combination of the thickness of her feather boa and a swipe of a broom from the quick thinking hall caretaker, Arnold Ramsbottom.

In fact, it took two brooms, eight handbags and the size 12 boot of the aforementioned Mr Ramsbottom to rid the hall of the feline felon. It proved twice as difficult to do the same with an equally irate and miffed Mrs Prudence Popplethwaite, who for some inexplicable reason insisted, nay demanded, that the judges 'do a recount.'

That night, as Patch lay in his basket reflecting on the lively events of the day, his tail involuntarily wagged in satisfaction. It was the end of a 'purrfect' day for the little terrier and nothing gave him more satisfaction – apart from sausages, of course, or Mistress Ma's gravy – than a battle won against the mean Mongolian monster.

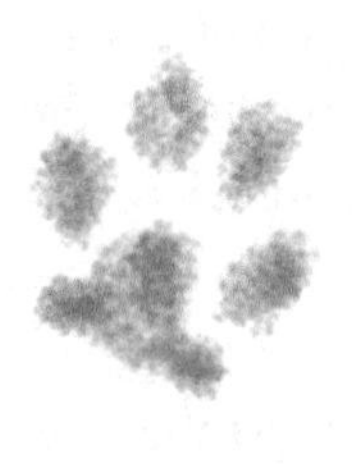

16

Top Dog

PATCH was not in a good mood. On one paw it was the biggest day for months, one that he had been eagerly waiting for – the Hillthorpe and Daleswick Dog Show final. What made it more special for Patch was that it would be the first time ever that the young Bedlington was going to take part.

On the other paw, whether he liked it or not, it meant something the terrier dreaded even more than listening to one of Reverend Sedgwick's sermons or finding the 'closed' sign on the door of Fishwick's butchers – a doggy bath!

'Now come on, Our Patch,' encouraged little Emma, 'yer have to look beautiful if yer want to impress the judges.'

While Tommy pressed down on his pet's haunches and Victor poured the cold, wet water over Patch's head and body, Emma rubbed in the soap.

Surprisingly that day there was not too much resistance from the little terrier, who understood that this ritual torture was a necessary evil in preparation for the big contest that every dog in the two villages were barking or meowing on about for the past few months. Patch stood there, paws firmly dug into terra firma, teeth clenched, as another jug of 'freezing' water drenched his coat of fur.

'For Dog's sake, get on with it,' thought Patch. 'I really don't see why I have to be so clean anyway; surely, my natural good looks, superb physique and great charm should be more than enough!' he reasoned.

Unfortunately his point of view was not shared by the three Wagstaff children, who appeared to him to relish their roles as 'terrier torturers'.

Neither was Patch's mood improved when young Edward, who up until then had been missing all the fun, came down the road after visiting his friend Percy Jowitt from a few doors up. Seeing the family pet's newly shining coat, which thanks to some expert teasing from the comb of Emma, was puffed up like a summer's cloud drifting across the North Yorkshire skies, Edward announced to his siblings and fellow pack member: 'By 'eck Patch, I don't know if thee will win best dog in show but I reckon yer 'ave a good chance in any best sheep contest.'

All the children laughed but their merriment was not shared by Patch.

This remark infuriated the sensitive Bedlington, who thought it was bad enough to be mocked by his mate Slipper, who had made a similar quip once before after one of his previous 'tortures', but to be made fun of by a fellow member of the Wagstaff pack was all too much!

Patch barked his disapproval, backed away from his 'captors' and much to the consternation of little Emma, went into 'hyperdoggy' shake, and in doing so soaked all the children in one frenzied outpouring of his obvious indignation.

However, the damage was already done. It was too late and there was not much Patch could do – he just had to accept that he had to depend on his supreme physical condition and evident good looks to secure the title.

'There's no point in fighting nature,' thought Patch. 'Bedlingtons, thank Dog, are definitely blessed when it comes to beauty and brains. It's a deadly combination.'

Indeed, if the winner of the canine section of the Hillthorpe and Daleswick Dog Show was judged on modestly alone – then Patch would not have had a dog's chance.

Fortunately for the highly opinionated terrier the judges were looking for more tangible qualities. Although it was not registered as an official Kennel Club show and all breeds – and indeed, 'cross breeds' took part – it was nevertheless, a keenly contested event, not just by the pet owners but by their animals themselves.

There were three stages where each dog was assessed by the Hillthorpe and Daleswick Dog Show judges – physical appearance, a combination of alertness and intelligence and finally, and very importantly, obedience.

The night before the show, when the Wagstaffs were gathered together for their evening meal around the kitchen table for one of Ma's delicious Yorkshire stews, the topic of conversation was naturally the next day's dog show.

'It's a pity there's not a doggy disobedience class. Our Patch would walk it,' quipped Victor.

All the two pawed Wagstaffs chuckled and nodded in agreement. Patch responded with a doggy frown and a little whimper at such an unfair comment but quickly ignored it, concentrating instead on trying to acquire a drop of Ma's very tasty evening meal. He performed his whole 'begging' repertoire, from pleading, puppy eyes, 'shiver and whimper' to the more aggressive and demanding bark. Nothing worked. Ma was adamant – Patch would even say 'dogged' – that there would be no 'treats' for him that evening and he was on a 'doggy diet' until after the show.

'Our Patch must be in prime condition if 'e's going to beat that Mrs Curtois-Pughs and that cocky spaniel of hers, Archie,' announced Ma.

It wasn't normaly like his wife to be disrespectful to either woman or beast, so these remarks made Da smile.

'Eh, I didn't know 'ow much this dog show matters to yer pet,' he said.

'It didn't Da,' confided Ma, 'until earlier today when I went into Fishwick's and that awful Prudence Popplethwaite and equally loathsome Ethel Curtois-Pughs were there. When I came in they both turned their nose up in the air as if I wuz beneath them. They had nothin' better to do than gossip and then they had the gall to tell me that it wasn't worth Our Patch entering the show as Bedlingtons were not a recognised pedigree breed of dog by the Kennel Club and anyway, that only their precious Archie had the bearin' and poise of a true champion.

'I gave Curtois-Pughs and that Popplethwaite woman what for, I did,' continued a blatantly irritated Ma, much to the glee of the children and a bemused Da.

'I told her that their pathetic, spoiled, ill-behaved excuse of a mutt wasn't a patch on Our Patch and that her Archie yapped more than the pair of them put together. That shut them up and apart from a "Reeaally". . .' – Ma stuck her nose in the air and stressed each word for emphasis – 'from Mrs

Popplethwaite and a "How dare you!" from that Curtois – la de dah – Pughs, I didn't get another yap out of them.'

The children burst into applause and Da grinned before giving his wife a big kiss on her cheek, much to Ma's embarrassment.

Patch beamed with pride at his beloved Mistress leaping to his defence and defending his honour, before coming to the sad conclusion that even these wonderful words would not mean his chances of some Yorkshire stew had increased.

'My Dog,' thought Patch, 'If I knew I was going to be starved to death I wouldn't have entered the show in the first place.'

He sank to the ground in despair, realising there would be no stew forthcoming; he placed his snout in between his paws and let out a whine of frustration to announce his lamentable state of having a very empty stomach. Much to his chagrin he was completely ignored, having, according to the rest of the Wagstaffs, 'cried wolf' too many times before at the kitchen table.

It was a beautiful summer in the North Yorkshire dales that year of 1913 and the next day was a perfect July one to hold the much awaited Hillthorpe and Daleswick Dog Show.

The canine event was held in its usual venue of the village chapel hall, which perfectly for the show, had a large garden area to hold the judging – and much to the relief of exhibitors, their pets and the judges, it was an exceptionally warm day.

To the annoyance of Prudence Popplethwaite, the judging panel was made up of three fair and reputable people, who were not easily 'influenced' – the Reverend's wife Selma Sedgwick, local schoolteacher Euan Neilsen and mine foreman Sid Jessop.

'What do they know about good pedigree,' confided Mrs Popplethwaite to her chum Mrs Curtois-Pughs. 'They don't have an experienced eye like you or I to recognise how a superior canine is structured, or if it walks with an acceptable gait.'

Mrs Curtois-Pughs condescended a slight knowing nod of her head to acknowledge agreement before replying: 'One cannot say one is worried too much, my dear; even the most inexperienced of judges could not fail to recognise the evident bloodline of my adorable Archie – I believe he can trace his ancestral roots not just to King Charles the second but all the way back to William the Conqueror.'

It was an outrageous statement, even by Mrs Curtois-Pughs' standards, but Mrs Popplethwaite would not be put off her stride.

'William the Conqueror, that is very impressive, Mrs Curtois-Pughs; for your dog to have such a regal lineage,' she replied before trumping her friend with, 'Of course, my cat Genghis goes back way further than that French king. His ancestors were from the cats of the court of Emperor Genghis Khan, you know, who at that time conquered half the known civilised world.'

Mrs Curtois-Pughs raised an eyebrow in surprise and a puzzled look at her fellow tabby, but wisely kept her counsel to herself.

History was not Prudence Popplethwaite's forte.

There was no doubt about it – despite Patch's reluctance at the children's attempts to wash him – the end result impressed both Ma and Emma, his two sternest judges when it came to appearances.

'By 'eck, Our Patch, yer don't 'alf scrub up well,'

beamed Ma, 'yer be the 'ansomest dog there today. That's fer sure.'

The lovely Emma also demonstrated her approval by going down on her knees, wrapping her slim arms around the little terrier and giving him a big kiss, smack on top of his tuft.

Patch almost squirmed with embarrassment at this public display of female affection – especially in front of his 'brothers'. He remembered seeing Victor once equally distraught. Ma was called to the school when her boy had fallen off a wall. It turned out not to be a broken bone but a bruised shoulder; however, fearing something worse, a relieved Ma gave Victor an unexpected hug in front of his mates. Victor didn't know what was more embarrassing – the sharp pain in his shoulder or being kissed by his mother in front of the whole class.

What compounded his 'pain' was that he was called 'mummy's boy' at school for a week until, not being able to contain his emotions any longer, he punched his final accuser, Ivor Tuttle, right on the nose.

Well, it was just how Patch was feeling now, like his fellow pack member on that occasion – 'the sooner this dog show is over the better', as far as he was concerned, so he could go and roll in the mud to his heart's content.

'Why couldn't they just give me the trophy now,' thought Patch. 'It would save a lot of disappointment for the other dogs!'

At that moment Patch even began to feel sorry for that snooty Archie but one flick of a dog's tail later the image of Mrs Curtois-Pughs' cocker spaniel came to his mind. He growled at the mere thought of his nemesis.

'No. My winning will serve that Archie right – a bit of public humiliation will do that excuse for a dog the world of good. Why, I never knew such a self-opinionated, selfish, self-centred creature in all my life;' concluded Patch, 'he doesn't half fancy himself!

'Mind you, he doesn't need taking down a peg or two, he's short enough already!'

It was a catty remark, which normally a dog like Patch would consider below him, but any mention of Archie always brought the worst out of the terrier.

'Come on, Patch,' called Tommy. 'It's time for t'show.'

Mistress Ma, Young Master Tommy and Young Mistress Emma turned to the front door as Patch got up on his paws from his basket and obediently followed – ready for the dogfight!

Reluctantly Patch allowed Master Tommy to put him on the lead for the show – a 'necessary evil' as far as he was concerned.

They all walked down the cobbled street towards the church hall where the registration for the dog show competition was about to take place.

The Wagstaffs arrived at the hall to a scene of organised chaos, as more than 30 dogs of all breeds and of all shapes and sizes, complete with their owners – of all shapes and sizes – gathered for the big event.

Patch scanned the hall to quickly assess the opposition before he joined the queue with the other Wagstaffs to register with the dog show secretary, Ernie Tapper.

It was a long wait, as each dog had to be individually numbered, whilst the owners gave their details and a small registration fee was collected.

Patch wiled away the time by making acquaintance with Hamish, a Scottish border terrier, and having a 'bow-wow' about who was the better football team – Newcastle United or Glasgow Rangers. Not that Patch, or Hamish, had seen a professional football match, but both heard their young masters enthusing about the subject and came to their own conclusions.

Of course, Patch's favourite football team of all time was the Bedlington Terriers. He had heard of this wonderful side when enjoying a 'kick about' with Edward and Victor on the Slag Heap. The latter was impressed by a 'header' from Patch and complimented him by saying: 'Eh, Our Patch, yer that good yer be playing for Bedlington Terriers one day.

Patch could only dream.

Patch enjoyed meeting a new friend in Hamish but conceded he 'dinnae' understand half of the conversation with him because of the Scottish border terrier's heavy Glaswegian accent.

'He may as well as come from Sunderland; he don't 'alf talk funny, does that Hamish,' thought Patch. Unbeknown to the Bedlington his Scottish 'cousin' was reiterating exactly the same thoughts at that very moment – substituting the words 'Hamish' with 'Patch' and 'Sunderland' with 'Aberdeen'.

At last it was the Wagstaffs' turn to register their pet and Ernie Tapper greeted them all with a warm smile and patted Patch on the tuft.

'Good afternoon, Mrs Wagstaff. Glad to see your Patch entering our little competition this year. First time for him, isn't it?' politely inquired Ernie, who was a fellow miner and knew Da well.

'Yes it is Ernie. I think 'e's been lookin' forward to it but we're a bit worried about the obedience class,' confided Ma.

Ernie laughed. 'Don't worry. 'E's obviously an intelligent animal is your Patch. I think I'm not too bad a judge of dogs and if yer ask me yer got a good un there, Mrs Wagstaff. I'm sure 'ee'll pick it up quickly. Besides 'e's obviously got good breeding – just like his owner. Now just fill out this form and it'll be sixpence for his entry fee.'

Ma almost blushed at Ernie's gracious but unexpected compliment and was just about to complete the registration form when there was a big clatter as the doors of the village hall were pushed open. In came a slim, nervous young man carrying a dog basket, complete with cushions, noticeably stitched with the personal monogram of ACP. He was followed by Mrs Curtois-Pughs herself, making an entrance and carrying in her arms 'her baby', Archie.

Mrs Curtois-Pughs held her chin up and breezed past the line-up of would-be contestants, completely ignoring the howls of protest from both humans and hounds, before proceeding to the head of the registration table to 'announce' hers and her pet's arrival to the dog secretary.

Without even allowing the surprised secretary to utter one word she informed him: 'Since my Archie is the reigning, supreme champion I see no need to waste my time with the minutiae of petty form filling. Besides, you already have all our details from last year.'

But even before Ernie could make a sound she had nodded her command to her 'man' carrying her dog basket and this poor, unfortunate nephew – dragooned into service for the day, against his will – took out the sixpence entry fee and put it down on the secretary's table.

The 'formalities', as far as Mrs Curtois-Pughs was concerned, were over and although Ernie tried to stop her, she turned and flounced off, looking to find a suitable spot for her Archie to 'rest'.

A dazed Ernie was almost left speechless by her arrogance as manservant, mutt and mistress ignored his attempts to follow the proper procedure.

Safe in the arms of his mistress, Archie looked down from high at Patch on the hall floor and yapped his disapproval before sticking his tongue out at him. Patch growled at his old adversary for the sheer rudeness of such an 'undoggedly' gesture.

'Come Archie, my precious,' trilled Mrs Curtois-Pughs. 'Do not let that beastly little Bedlington frighten you. Mummy's here. He's only trying to upset you. Take no notice my baby.'

With that she commanded: 'You may continue now, Tapper,' before instructing her nephew to place the basket near an open window – so Archie was not sweltering.

Ernie Tapper, an honest, down to earth miner, was not pleased with this unnecessary and haughty behaviour from Mrs Curtois-Pughs but with more than 25 other dogs to register he swallowed his pride and continued to process the other entrants.

Once the formalities were over, Ernie banged the table for attention and announced to all assembled: 'Will entrants and their owners now proceed please, to the hall garden to begin the first inspection by the judges? Thank you.'

He paused before adding: 'Er, Mrs Curtois-Pughs, may I have a word with you please?'

His friendly request elicited a frosty response from Mrs

C-P and even a yap of disapproval from the little dog she cradled in her arms. She glared back in protest at such an imposition on her precious time.

'Really Tapper, is this at all necessary? Archie and I must focus our energies for the competition,' she dismissively replied.

Before the bemused dog secretary could reply, the object of his 'inquisition' was distracted by something 'far more important' in her mind when the three show judges arrived through the hall entrance – so Mrs C-P decided to rudely ignore the 'obviously over officious official' and 'focused her energies' to greet them instead.

Although Mrs Sedgwick, Mr Neilsen and Mr Jessop were, in her mind, clearly below her social status, at that moment Mrs C-P suddenly saw them in a completely different light. She brushed aside the 'protestations' of an ignored Tapper and practically glided across the hall floor towards the judges, putting her smile onto full beam.

'How marvellous to meet you,' she gushed – obviously more pleased to see the three officials than they were to see her at that moment.

'It is so reassuring that the vitally important task of deciding the next Hillthorpe and Daleswick Dog Show champion is in the capable hands of your esteemed selves.

'Of course, I would not have entered my own little champion Archie again if this show did not have such an excellent reputation among the canine owners' community for its continuing high standards,' she flattered.

Sid Jessop, a first time adjudicator but chosen as a 'fair and honest man', soon made Mrs C-P regret her opening gambit. 'Fair and honest men' were a poor choice in her eyes then, say, compared to much more 'flexible' judges, such as last year when Prudence Popplethwaite was their chief.

'Nice little King Charles cross yer got there pet,' Sid politely responded before he made the mistake of patting Archie on his little domed head.

Accusing her Archie of being a 'cross' only made the creature's owner more cross.

The creature reacted with a yap, followed by a snarl, bearing his teeth. It was not a pretty sight. Sid quickly withdrew his hand of friendship.

'My Archie is a pedigree working cocker spaniel,' bellowed its owner, emphasising the word 'pedigree' in an exasperated tone – clearly not impressed by Sid Jessop's judging 'pedigree'.

It took two chocy drops from 'mummy' to calm the shredded nerves of the reigning show champion.

With all the registration appearing to be complete, humans and hounds were ushered out into the garden for the preliminary judging. It was quite a sight as the 30 dogs and their owners lined up for inspection.

Ernie Tapper was just about to conclude the registration when, once again, for the second time that day, the doors of the hall burst dramatically open.

It was a sight that many in Hillthorpe would have gladly paid good money to see. Bounding in at a rate of knots was a big, beautiful bouncy Irish wolfhound, whose fur of striking red/ginger colour, matched the hair of many a native of the Emerald Isle.

With its tongue hanging out and a roguish glint in its eye, the handsome hound immediately reminded Patch of his good friend Slipper – if not the handsome bit. Slipper, of course, was not present at the dog show because it meant he would have been in danger of having to sit still for more than 30 seconds at one time.

The strapping Irish wolfhound came to a halt right in front of Ernie Tapper, as if instinctively he knew where to stop.

'Quite an impressive entrance for a stranger,' thought Patch.

But even more impressive for the intrigued onlookers, was that lady attached to the end of the dog's lead, stumbling to keep up with the energetic canine Hibernian; it was no less than Mrs Prudence Popplethwaite herself – panting and puffing and obviously relieved that her 'charge' had eventually come to a halt as she tried to regain her breath from her recent exertions.

'Rory, sit. There's a good boy,' commanded the obviously flustered Mrs P. It was an instruction given so that all in the hall would be in no doubt who was in charge. It was also an unnecessary instruction as Rory had been sitting patiently already for twenty seconds while 'his owner' regathered her composure.

'I am sure, Mr Tapper, that we are not late for the registration for the dog show,' trilled the now more composed Mrs Popplethwaite. It was more of a command than a request.

'No, Mrs Popplethwaite. You have just made it,' replied the obliging dog show secretary. 'Looks like your dog is anxious to be on time. I can see you didn't 'ave to drag him here Mrs, like some of the entrants.

'I thought I knew all the dogs around Hillthorpe and Daleswick. Is this yer new pet Mrs Popplethwaite?'

His remark did not impress the village gossip one bit and

she ignored his opening 'unnecessary' comments. However, she was eager to let everyone know where this strange dog had come from and why she was entering the animal at the last minute.

'Oh, this wonderful specimen is not mine Mr Tapper. He belongs to. . .' (there was then a slight pause for dramatic effect and her voice began to rise to make a more public proclamation) . . .'Lord Swelldale.'

Mrs Popplethwaite had expected at least a gasp of surprise and envy from those within earshot – although she did take some satisfaction from seeing Mrs Curtois-Pughs raise an eyebrow.

She continued: 'Lord Swelldale could not be here himself today as he has a far more important engagement to attend to but he has appointed me as his representative.'

There was certainly no hint of modesty as she proudly 'confided', whether the dog show secretary was interested or not: '"Mrs Popplethwaite," Lord Swelldale said to me the other day, "I could not think of anyone better than your good self to represent me, nor could my Rory be in better hands." '

What Mrs Popplethwaite had failed to mention was a ten-month letter campaign to the aforementioned Lord 'on behalf of the Hillthorpe and Daleswick Dog Show committee', virtually begging the poor (well, not so poor) man to 'graciously enter one of his fine pedigree hounds in the event, allowing his esteemed name, prestige and patronage to become attached to such a humble show.'

Against his better judgement, in a bid to avoid further 'social harassment' from this 'dreadful woman', the twelfth letter finally broke the peer's resolve and he begrudgingly agreed to 'allow' one of his dogs to enter – on condition that:

A) He would not be expected to attend and B) He would never have to enter one of his dogs ever again.

'Of course,' announced Mrs Popplethwaite, not just to the show secretary, 'Lord Swelldale would not be too pleased if you refused his prime pedigree entry. . .'

It was another unnecessary comment, for Ernie Tapper was only too pleased for any hound, from whatever bloodline, to enter, and handed Rory's 'owner', Mrs Popplethwaite, a pencil to complete a form.

Ma stood by, clearly irritated by Mrs Popplethwaite's pompous attitude. So in an equally loud voice, for the ears of all, especially her old adversary, she said to Tommy.

'I was only saying to King George the other day there's one thing I cannot stand; and do you know what he said to me, Tommy?'

A bemused Tommy looked at his mother strangely before asking, 'What's that Ma?'

'You know George, the one thing I can't stand most is. . . name dropping.'

Ma continued:

' "Name dropping," replied King George to me. "I could not agree with you more, Ma. Nothin' worse." '

Everyone in the hall burst out laughing, especially a grinning Ernie Tapper – all except Prudence Popplethwaite, of course, who put on her most royal 'One is not amused' look.

Emma, clearly impressed, tugged at her mother's skirt, looking up with wide adoring eyes, before whispering, 'I didn't know you know His Majesty the King, Ma?'

Ma smiled at her innocence and kissed her on the head.

Mrs Popplethwaite's cause was not helped when she

tugged Rory's lead and walked imperiously towards the garden. Her advance was halted when the gigantic wolfhound refused to budge and she was jerked backwards and almost lost her footing – much to the amusement of those present. A second, two-handed tug, did the trick and Mrs Popplethwaite left after giving a snooty 'Hmmph' aimed towards Ma, as she pulled on the lead with all her might to 'guide' Rory to the sanctuary of the garden.

'Come along, m'lord,' she instructed her 'pet'. 'Take no notice of this riff-raff.'

Diplomacy or good humour was not among Prudence Popplethwaite's fortes.

There could not have been a more perfect day for such an event as the sun basked down on dogs, owners, judges, stewards and spectators, who all anticipated an equally splendid show. They were not to be disappointed.

An assortment of breeds lined up with their owners for the first inspection by the three officials. Long and short legged, muscular and 'whippet' thin, shaggy and smooth haired – and that was before the dogs present were taken into consideration.

But it was not just the physical appearances of the entrants – there were all sorts of temperaments to observe. Mollie, the laid back Alsatian, was just happy to lay down in the sun and be next to her friend Jess, a black Labrador; while Jess herself was content to flirt with Rory, the good looking, aristocratic stranger in town.

Patch himself just rested on his behind, smartly and attentively next to Young Master – ready to impress the judges who were slowly coming down the line towards him with their clipboards and pencils in hand.

A couple of dogs down from Patch was Panther, the greyhound, who the terrier earmarked for a 'top three' finish – two positions behind himself of course!

Naturally Mrs Popplethwaite, with lead and Rory firmly in hand, had positioned herself next to her friend Mrs Curtois-Pughs and Archie.

Archie began to yap – his natural instinct – having to suffer the double indignity of, for the first time that day, being left on the ground with all the other dogs, which merely, especially standing next to the Irish wolfhound, highlighted his diminutive stature; secondly, there was the insult of the judges keeping him waiting.

Following the preliminary inspection each owner was asked to 'parade' their dog in front of the assembled multitude.

After much deliberation – well not so much by Sid Jessop, who had already made up his mind straight away – more on the part of Mr Neilsen and Mrs Sedgwick – the six finalists were chosen.

'The six finalists are,' announced chief judge, Mrs Sedgwick, without pomp or ceremony, 'Hamish, Panther, Gorse, Archie, Patch and Rory.'

There was a polite round of applause from the humans present and the odd bark of approval from some of the more gracious dogs who were not chosen among the elite half dozen.

The first dog for the final round was Hamish, who impressed with his no-nonsense, determined and almost military bearing as he marched across the 'parade ground'.

Patch and his new-found friend Hamish admire Rory, the Irish wolfhound.

Next up was Panther, who moved beautifully, with speed, aggression and was not lacking in grace. He was followed by Gorse, the beautiful black Labrador, who with his shiny coat and friendly countenance, was bound to score high marks.

The dog show was, indeed, fulfilling its promise of canine excellence, until the entrance – or put perhaps in a kinder way, the brief appearance – of finalist number four.

'Mrs Prudence Popplethwaite and 'Rory' please step forward,' boomed Mr Neilsen as if reaching the back of his class at the junior school.

For one brief moment Mrs Popplethwaite appeared to have finally mastered (or mistressed) the technique of having the Irish wolfhound in a semblance of being under some control. Mrs P strolled to the centre of the 'arena' with her head erect, nose in the air, ample bosom protruding and her short, stubby, bow-legs giving her the gait of a drunken sailor on his first night in port. Her movement and figure were in great contrast to the more elegant and graceful figure of the one she led 'in rein'.

As one unkind, but not inaccurate observer, commented (Bert Dyson), it was 'like a clapped out, ancient pit pony leading a virile Arab stallion in its prime.'

It took all of Mrs Popplethwaite's willpower to suppress her natural instincts not to give a 'Royal wave' to the crowd – she was, after all, in her mind, representing the top echelon of society. 'No doubt Lord Swelldale would have been very proud of me,' she thought to herself at that moment.

Her moment in the sun, however, was shattered by, no less, her own 'beloved'. For, from the safe distance of a nearby shed roof observing the dog show proceedings with vehement disdain was her cat Genghis – seeing his mistress making a complete fool of herself, again, was bad enough but fraternising with the 'canine enemy' doubly rubbed salt into his wounds.

If Genghis had three eyes, one of them would have been, no doubt, one of the 'green-eyed' monster variety.

The Mongolian cross, who had his own moment of glory snatched away from him by that 'despicable Patch' was now hell bent on revenge – and was only too happy to spoil the dog show – especially if it upset a few of his canine adversaries.

To register his disapproval Genghis miaowed and spat and hissed; he scratched the top of the shed roof with his claws to make as much noise as possible to make his protest manifest – until 'the Evil One' stole the attention he craved and had every dog in the show barking its disapproval. Provocatively, he even had the temerity to jump down from the shed roof and into the edge of the garden itself – causing a near frenzy amongst the dogs, who all had, up to that point, been so well-behaved.

Patch, not so easily fooled by Genghis's antics, refused to take the bait and stood alert but firm at Tommy's side – knowing that a break down in discipline – surely Genghis's purpose – would mean dogtastrophe.

The 'new dog in town', Rory, was not so sanguine and reacted how any red – or in his case blue – blooded hound would have at the sight of a cantankerous cat, deciding to charge after the unwelcome intruder in hot pursuit.

Unfortunately Rory had not made his intentions clear to his 'owner' and in one majestic moment of madness the wolfhound bounded towards the malignant Mongolian with the unaware Mrs P holding tightly at the end of the lead – there was only one possible outcome.

From one minute proudly leading her charge in centre field, Mrs Popplethwaite suddenly found herself yanked off her feet at a rate of knots in a completely different direction. In vain, she tried desperately to retain her foothold as Rory scampered powerfully across the lawn towards his prey.

Much to the secret delight of the crowd Mrs P spun around at 180 degrees, reluctantly in frantic pursuit of her own pet.

Before she could even utter the command: 'Rory, no. . !' her strangulated plea soon turned into one continuous word – 'Rornooooah!'

With the wolfhound gathering pace the entertained crowd watched the staggering figure of a now hatless Prudence Popplethwaite, completely swept off her feet as the twisted lead wrapped itself around her podgy little fingers and wrist. The result was she now found herself being dragged along the ground with an energised Rory ignoring her desperate pleas for him to halt.

For Genghis everything was going to plan in his bid to disrupt, if not ruin, the dog show. The febrile feline stood just long enough to entice the hot headed and fast approaching Rory (with Mrs P in tow) towards him; it was also just long enough to avoid any danger of being caught, before the wily cat decided to scarper through a handy hole in the hedge – just enough room for him but not enough for the 'stupid dog'.

However, what Genghis had not calculated was Rory's determination. This mere obstacle was not enough to put off the intrepid Irish hero and he leapt over the four foot high greenery in one athletic bound – giving a fresh surge of momentum to the attached Mrs P at the end of his lead.

At last 'the ride from hell' was over for Hillthorpe's most

prolific gossip, as Rory came to a halt 20 yards later when Genghis scampered up the safety of a convenient tree (escape plan B for the fiendish tactician) leaving Rory at its base, barking in frustration. Genghis spat and hissed and glared in triumph at the dog's impotence.

This end of hostilities, which was over barring the barking and hissing, allowed Mrs P to untangle herself from the leather leash, much to her relief – and Rory's.

She staggered, battered and bruised, back to the showground. Much to her credit she still had his Lordship's prize hound in hand – if not entirely under full control. Both panted heavily after their exertions.

'Eh, our Mrs P,' commented a cheeky Bert Dyson, 'Yer look like yer have been pulled through a hedge backwards!'

Even Ma and Emma could not suppress a giggle.

Sid Jessop gallantly picked up Mrs Popplethwaite's abandoned hat and returned it to its owner.

She snatched the hat from his hand without a word of thanks, before spitting out a twig from her mouth.

Regaining her composure she declared: 'His Lordship, Lord Swelldale, has instructed me to withdraw his entry from the Hillthorpe and Daleswick Dog Show forthwith.'

She then tottered away with Rory 'in tow' towards the church hall and an inglorious exit.

It was a remarkable display of trying to restore her self-dignity after such blatant public humiliation. It was a performance worthy of England at its best – a stiff upper lip to adversity that had forged a British Empire.

Ma almost admired the woman.

'Ladies and gentlemen, and dogs,' announced Mrs Sedgwick, breaking the silence and eager to continue, 'the dog show will now continue. Will Archie now take to the centre?'

It was the moment that Archie and Mrs Curtois-Pughs had been waiting for, and anticipating for the past 12 months – even though the build-up, especially after Mrs Popplethwaite's spectacle, was not in Mrs C-P's opinion 'ideal'.

However, if Mrs Curtois-Pughs could have dreamed of a better presentation by her beloved pet then it would have been hard to top her little darling's performance at the Hillthorpe and Daleswick Dog Show that day.

Archie, the reigning supreme champion, was at his most supreme – with his attendant 'in tow' (in sharp contrast to the previously demonstrated 'in tow' by a certain Mrs Popplethwaite/Rory combination), the cocker spaniel enthralled judges and onlookers alike, using all his experience and skills with a faultless display of 'canine chic' as if he had stepped off a Parisian catwalk (or as Patch would have said, dog walk).

The cocker spaniel was at his cockiest and most coquettish – flouncing, bouncing and strutting to charm the most stone-hearted judge. He even went on his hind legs, raised his paws about his chest and whimpered for maximum effect – it was 'cuteness' personified. His speciality of 'play dead and suddenly come alive again' (which helped to win last year's title) was brought out of his bottom draw, in response to a well-rehearsed 'command' from Mrs Curtois-Pughs; who trilled 'Where's mummy?' before a near death Archie sprang to life, ran to his 'mummy' and planted a big, sloppy kiss on her cheek with his little tongue. It elicited several 'oohs and aahs' from the more gullible in the audience.

Patch looked on, mustering all his self-discipline not to be 'doggy sick' at such a blatantly, undoggedly display of such uninhibited sycophancy to crowd please. If dogs could flutter their eyelashes and blow kisses at the judges then Archie would have no hesitation in doing so.

Archie's 'piece de resistance' was a double pirouette on his hind legs – it was his personal tribute to the famous Russian ballerina, Anna Pavlova, which ended, auspiciously, with his own version of 'the dying swan'.

The crowd burst out in applause.

Mrs Curtois-Pughs clapped her hands in awe at such a sublime performance by her beloved 'Archipoos'.

'You were simply divine, my darling,' she gushed to her 'little soldier'.

It was not quite the sentiments Patch and some of the other village dogs held at that particular moment, who were all somewhat embarrassed at this insult to dogginess.

'Woofter,' thought Patch, although slightly worried at the lowliness the competition could stoop to, in order to secure the crown. 'If they knew what I knew about what that excuse for a dog is really like I'd. . .'

The Bedlington did not have time to extend his thoughts because, with Rory 'withdrawn' from the competition, Mrs Sedgwick now called Patch to take centre stage.

'Showtime!' he muttered to himself. 'If they want cute, I'll show them cute,' and he pulled Tommy by his lead to take his place in the gladiatorial arena.

Once settled in the ring Tommy took the lead off and the 'show' began as all eyes turned on the final finalists.

The terrier's opening gambit to the three judges was inspirational. He walked over firstly to Mr Neilsen and then to Mr Jessop, stretching out his front paws towards them individually before making a slight bow. To the leading judge, Mrs Sedgwick, Patch went a little further in his boldness and after he bowed, the entranced lady held out her hand and the little dog leant over to 'kiss' the back of it with a soft lick in the most gentlemanly of fashions. Mrs Sedgwick was charmed, as were the spectators, some of whom gave a few 'aahs' in appreciation.

The general acknowledgement was not shared by the petulant Archie, who now safely ensconced in the arms of his mistress, looked down in disdain while thinking: 'Dognation, why didn't I think of that?'

Archie's frown lines came to eminence, matching those of his equally petulant owner.

Patch now had the expectant spectators in his paws and made his next crowd pleasing move. In a rehearsed manoeuvre he had practised in fun with Young Master only the night before, he jumped up so his front paws were lying on Tommy's chest. With his back paws firmly planted on the top of his Young Master's shoes the pair began to 'dance' on the grass – bringing further 'oohs and aahs – especially from the females in the audience.

'I think it's a fox-hound-trot,' quipped Bert Tyson, which added to the merry atmosphere.

'Could be a Patchadouble,' added Sid Jessop, with a big grin to elicit more laughs.

But the Bedlington was not finished yet – he could not match Archie's 'Dying Swan' act – nor would he want to – there was, however, a magnificent climax to his truly memorable performance.

Patch withdrew about 20 feet away from his Young

Master. Tommy then dug the back of his right heel into the ground just before him to give himself a firm anchor; he then braced himself, took a deep breath before giving his young dog an encouraging 'Here boy.' Patch's ears stood erect as he responded to the signal and he ran like the wind towards his master. The crowd was hushed, not knowing what to expect. From just a couple of feet away Patch suddenly leaped into the air to plant two paws firmly, but gently, on his master's chest, using it as a springboard to do a backflip and rotating 360 degrees in the air before landing elegantly on his four paws.

It was a manoeuvre the famous German aerial 'dogfighter' Baron von Richthofen would have been proud of in the years to come. It was a manoeuvre Patch himself named 'the Skye terrier'.

The audience burst out into spontaneous applause and even all the dogs, well, all except a certain working cocker spaniel, howled their approval at such daring dog-do.

Patch had often 'performed' the same 'Skye terrier' on the Slag Heap many an afternoon in play with Young Master but never before with such skill and aplomb. Encouraged, the Bedlington then ran round in a circle to attempt the gymnastic display again and again it was perfectly executed and again, the crowd voiced, clapped and barked their approval.

Archie and Mrs Curtois-Pughs looked on stony-faced. Were they about to lose their coveted and rightful crown to this 'pesky mongrel usurper?'

Mrs C-P's nephew and attendant stood reverentially on hand, a step behind Archie and his 'mistress', ready to administer, on command, an emergency 'chocy-drop'. Now it was down to the judges, who retired to the church hall to confer, while owners, dogs and supporters went into a 'bow-wow of their own to reflect on the merits and weaknesses of each individual entrant and to speculate and give opinions on who would be 'top dog' that year.

Unlike the counterpart judging of the cat show, the dog show officials, led by the capable and no fuss Mrs Sedgwick, did not prolong proceedings any longer than they could help and after just a couple of minutes the three reappeared to announce the result.

'I'd like to thank all the entrants today – dogs and owners, spectators, my fellow judges Mr Neilsen and Mr Jessop and especially the show secretary Mr Tapper for making this such a grand show.

'All the contestants were marvellous and we judges had a very hard decision to make, especially when it came to the finalists. However, we have come to that decision.'

The crowd hushed to hear the verdict.

'In third place,' continued the chief judge, 'are our Scottish friends Hamish and his owner, Mr McTavish.'

There was polite applause as Mr McTavish stepped forward to receive their prizes of a rosette and a 2s 6d voucher, courtesy of Fishwick's Butchers.

Archie, safe in the hands of his mistress, looked down at his fellow competitor Patch with a look of superiority. The object of his scorn emitted a low, throaty growl. Tommy shook his lead and told him to 'behave.'

Mrs Sedgwick continued: 'In second place – and I must say the judges were split when it came to the top two – is. . . Patch, owned by Tommy Wagstaff.'

Patch could not believe his ears. 'Second,' he thought,

'I've never been second before in my life. I'm a Bedlington. It's an outrage. I'm easily the best looking here and no dog came anywhere near my Skye terrier,' he bemoaned. 'Second!'

The little terrier felt a sickening sensation in the pit of his stomach – it was as if, to him, Mr Fishwick had announced he would not been making sausages anymore. It was the end of the world!

But there was even worse news to come for Patch than 'the end of the world'.

Reluctantly and head bowed, and not even hearing the sympathetic cheers of the appreciative crowd, Patch was 'dragged' forward by Young Master to collect their prize – a shiny rosette and a five shilling voucher from Fishwick's was scant consolation.

Tommy, though, was 'well chuffed' with his prize, although Ma, who tried not to show it in front of the children, was disappointed because she dreaded the next announcement which would, most certainly, ruin her day.

'Finally,' announced Mrs Sedgwick, 'and we all agree what a splendid little dog he is, the winner of this year's Hillthorpe and Daleswick Dog Show, the Swelldale Cup and a ten shilling voucher from Fishwick's Butchers, our generous show sponsor, is. . . Archie, owned by Mrs Curtois-Pughs.'

At that moment all Patch wanted to do was dig a deep pit in the earth with his big paws and bury himself in it – just like the one he dug in the 'vegetable patch' with the odd treasured bone that Ma sometimes gave him from Fishwick's. He could just about take being beaten by Hamish, Panther, Molly, or even Slipper, but to lose to that excuse for a proper dog, Archie, it was more than a Bedlington could bear!

There were a few murmurs in the crowd from people who obviously felt the cocker spaniel did not deserve to retain his title but they did respect the decision as there was 'no' question of 'compliance' among the three respected and well-liked judges.

A beaming Mrs Curtois-Pughs, with her little hero cradled in her arms, moved, almost regally, to collect her spoils.

As Archie condescended to look down at Patch – sticking out his tongue at him, most undoggedly – at the same time, Mrs Curtois-Pughs could not resist a gloating glare at Ma, virtually the same action as her ill-mannered pooch but, of course, Mrs C-P was far too 'lady like' to repeat such a low, common vulgarity.

As she shifted Archie across to lay his little head in her shoulder and secured it safely with one hand, she 'graciously' put out the other to collect the coveted trophy. Unfortunately for the victor and victrix of the games in their moment of triumph, fate intervened – or rather a tap on Mrs Sedgwick's shoulder by Ernie Tapper, just as she was about to hand over the Swelldale Cup – albeit rather reluctantly – to an eager and poised Mrs Curtois-Pughs.

'I'm sorry Mrs Sedgwick. I can't let this go on any longer. Could I 'ave a quick word with you before yer make the presentation,' said the dog show secretary politely but firmly.

He whispered into the chief judge's ear and immediately a look of shock was seen on the face of the reverend's wife by all gathered.

'Oh my. . .' uttered a clearly perturbed Mrs Sedgwick, who then hurriedly gathered her fellow judges together for an 'on the spot' conference.

An equally stunned Mrs C-P, clearly irritated at this

'unnecessary interruption' to the anointing of her beloved champion, was heard to proclaim: 'Well, really. . .'

It also brought about a couple of irritating yaps from Archie.

'Ladies and gentlemen,' announced a clearly embarrassed Mrs Sedgwick, 'before we can hand over the cup to the winner, after receiving information from the dog show secretary of a breach of the rules, I have to declare, what they would say in dog racing circles – for which I'm sure many of you will understand – a 'steward's inquiry'.'

Mrs Curtois-Pughs was left open-mouthed and immediately there was uproar among the assembled as Mrs Sedgwick, Sid Jessop and Mr Neilsen, accompanied by Ernie Tapper, headed towards the sanctuary of the church hall to discuss the 'crisis'.

Even Ma was perplexed, while Patch himself was still in a state of mild shock and oblivious to proceedings.

'Me, a Bedlington, second to that, that. . .' he shuddered to think 'the unthinkable'.

A few moments later the show secretary came out of the hall and went over to Mrs Curtois-Pughs.

'Mrs Curtois-Pughs, would you please come in to talk to the judges? It will only take a moment,' he requested in a polite tone.

'Really Tapper,' spouted a clearly offended Mrs C-P, 'you have been unnecessarily pestering my Archie and one all day with your petty officialdom. I shall be making a formal complaint about your behaviour to your superiors, you mark my words.

'Interrupting our cup presentation, it really is too much,' she spat.

Archie added his 'two penneth worth' by snarling at Ernie and bearing his fangs at the target of his mounting frustration.

'If yer would like to come this way, Mrs Curtois-Pughs, all will be explained,' Ernie Tapper replied politely, refusing to respond to her vitriol and holding his hand up to guide her in the direction of the judges.

Once inside the hall Mrs Sedgwick did not beat about the bush, and without an ounce of pretence or sympathy told Mrs Curtois-Pughs: 'I'm afraid your Archie is disqualified, Mrs Curtois-Pughs.'

'Disqual. . .', blurted Mrs C-P, who could not even get the word out fully, such was her disbelief.

'For wh-aa-at?' she finally managed to utter.

'For not registering your entry of Archie properly,' replied Mrs Sedgwick.

Mrs Curtois-Pughs was opened-mouthed. Archie, for once, kept his shut.

'Despite many worthy attempts by Mr Tapper here to try and persuade you to complete the necessary forms, you blatantly ignored him. So, as you did not register, we cannot award you, or Archie, the prize. It would simply not be fair on all the other entries, who had taken their time to fill out their entries and followed the proper procedure,' Mrs Sedgwick informed her.

'But we paid our sixpence registration fee. My man. . . I mean my nephew. . . gave Tapper the money,' challenged an almost crimson faced Mrs Curtois-Pughs.

'Naturally,' countered Mrs Sedgwick, 'that will be returned to you.'

She nodded at Ernie Tapper and he immediately proffered

the aforementioned coin to Mrs C-P. Archie tried to bite his hand as he did so but was restrained by his owner, who, with a snort, refused the coin from the dog show secretary, before literally, turning on a sixpence to vent her indignation at such a humiliation.

However, she could not resist further comment and again, turned to face the judges.

'This is monstrous Mrs Sedgwick,' exclaimed Mrs Curtois-Pughs. 'You all have it in for Archie and one, just because you are my social inferiors.

'Tapper has been pestering me all day, trying to put us off. He obviously is prejudiced against us as you are too Selma Sedgwick – you are blatantly biased and jealous of our worthy success – both inside and outside the dog show arena.'

Mrs Sedgwick tried to conceal her anger after this latest riposte and her hackles clearly rose with this personal attack on herself, the two other judges and the amiable dog show secretary.

'I can assure you, Mrs Curtois-Pughs,' she retorted passionately but in a controlled fashion, 'that nobody in this room feels at least one bit inferior to you. And I can also assure you that if we were at all 'prejudiced' as you claim, why would we have chosen Archie as the winner?

'As for Mr Tapper pestering you, he was merely trying to do his job and, knowing you, Ethel Curtois-Pughs, if it comes to believing a hard-working, decent man like Ernie Tapper, or a stuck-up, gossip mongering, lazy lad-di-dah like you then I know which one I believe.'

While Ernie Tapper looked down on the floor in embarrassment at Mrs Sedgwick's testimony Sid Jessop grinned as he had not had such entertainment for years. He made a mental note to volunteer for judging duties again next year. Mr Neilsen was more used to witnessing barbarous behaviour as a veteran of the school playground.

Mrs Curtois-Pughs had refused to release her jaws from the 'dog fight'.

'Hmmmph. . .' she retorted. 'So if Tapper knew that I had not filled in the trifling forms properly why did you let Archie and I into the final, only for us to be dragged through this public humiliation and have the rightful crown snatched away in such cruel fashion? Or did you plan it that way all along Selma Sedgwick?

'For a former lass in the sorting sheds she certainly learned a few posh words,' thought Mrs Sedgwick.

The reverend's wife, not without some satisfaction, offered the floor to the dog show secretary.

'I think it's your turn to speak Ernie,' she said.

'Well the simple fact is, Mrs Curtois-Pughs, I really didn't want to mention this to you if I could 'elp it but, if you insist, I let it go so far 'cause I didn't think your Archie 'ad an hope in 'ell of winnin'.'

'Or even a cat's chance,' interjected Sid Jessop, warming to the occasion.

'I never expected him to make it to the final, let alone win it,' continued Ernie, making up for the time that Mrs C-P had not given him to speak.

Open-mouthed Mrs Curtois-Pughs could not believe what she was hearing.

'Let's face it Mrs,' said Ernie Tapper a little less respectfully. 'Yer only just got to look at that little yapper to know 'e hasn't got what it takes. 'E's certainly not a patch on that Patch or the rest of the finalists.'

'That's enough, Ernie,' interrupted the chief judge. 'I think Mrs Curtois-Pughs has got the picture.

'So why did you judges select my Archie as the winner, although it was naturally obvious?' came back the indignant newly disqualified. 'I'll tell you why – my little Archie was by far the best show dog out there and obviously the pick of the pedigrees.'

'I must admit he did very well, Mrs Curtois-Pughs,' said Mrs Sedgwick, 'but the reason Mr Neilsen and I voted for Archie, unlike Mr Jessop who maintained that he thought Patch the superior dog, was because we thought Patch overdid it with his gymnastic display. It is a dog show, after all, not a music hall act.

'Although,' she added, 'your Archie's 'dying swan' was unanimously agreed to be the funniest thing we have seen in ages and in the end he attracted our sympathy vote.'

It was not what Mrs Curtois-Pughs wanted to hear. She tried in vain to cover her baby's ears, fearing any more Archie heard could cause permanent psychological damage. Of course, it was far too late for that!

However, Mrs C-P was not a woman to go quietly with her tail between her legs.

'How dare you!' she screamed. 'How dare you! If you think you have heard the last of this you are very much mistaken. Call yourselves judges, you could not even run a. . .' – an incensed Mrs C-P was struggling for words – 'a. . . church bazaar.'

'Oh I think I have a pretty good record in that department, Mrs Curtois-Pughs, thank you,' assured the reverend's wife.

'I will make sure Lord Swelldale himself hears of how you treated his poor Rory and his representative Mrs

Popplethwaite,' before adding 'threateningly'. 'Don't you know who my husband is?'

' 'E's the chief clerk at the colliery Mrs Curtois-Pughs,' volunteered Mrs Sedgwick. 'Not Lord Asquith.'

'And another thing,' it was Mrs C-P's final salvo, 'I shall be informing the Kennel Club of my despicable treatment.'

'Please do,' said an incredulous Mrs Sedgwick, 'we are not affiliated to the Kennel Club. It's not Crufts lass, it's only the Hillthorpe and Daleswick Dog Show.'

Archie, of course, had the final yap as he and his owner, the latter ashen faced, stormed out in disgust from the church hall into the garden and out through the gate, ignoring the multitude gathered outside who were eagerly awaiting the 'verdict'.

The crowd did not have a clue what had just happened in the hall but it was certainly entertaining to see Mrs C-P and pet, along with her nephew scampering after them with basket in hand, disappearing into the distance – without the coveted trophy.

Immediately after, the judges and show secretary came out to 'reannounce' the winners.

'Owing to an administration error made by an entrant, the previous winners, Archie and Mrs Curtois-Pughs, have been disqualified,' announced Mrs Sedgwick.

Emma looked at Ma with wonderment.

She hugged Ma and said: 'That means Our Patch. . .' she was too excited to say anything more.

Ernie Tapper politely asked Tommy and Mr McTavish to hand back their prizes in the circumstances.

'So,' continued the chief judge, 'in third place is Gorse owned by Mary Tavy. There was warm applause as the rosette and voucher was presented to the genial Labrador and its owner.

'Second goes to Hamish and Mr McTavish.'

More polite applause as the judges congratulated the entry from across the border.

'And it gives me great pleasure,' continued the chief judge, 'to give you the winner of the 1913 Hillthorpe and Daleswick Dog Show, the Swelldale Cup and a ten shilling voucher from Fishwick's the butchers, to Patch, owned by Tommy Wagstaff.'

Patch's ears pricked up. He heard the words 'winner' and 'Patch' and 'Fishwick's'. The Bedlington barked in delight. From utter despondency he had gone to sheer joy.

'Never doubted it for a moment,' he thought. 'Top dog. Leader of the pack. Back of the net!'

Tommy stepped forward and shyly accepted the cup on Patch's behalf. The terrier was more interested in the ten shilling voucher, which Ma quickly took possession of.

'Good boy, Patch,' Ma said, tickling him on his ears and ruffling his tuft, 'that's my boy.'

It was Patch's proudest moment. There were more congratulations to come as the lovely Emma bent down and gave her favourite dog a big hug followed by a kiss on the nose.

That night as Patch laid on his blanket, he eyed the little silver cup on top of the mantlepiece and reflecting back on the day his heart swelled with pride. Thinking of swelling, his stomach almost burst after the extra ration of Fishwick's finest which Mistress Ma had rewarded him with that evening.

'No more doggy diets until next year,' declared Patch to himself.

'Poor old Archie. It could not have happened to a more deserving dog,' he mused before dropping off to 'Doggy heaven'.

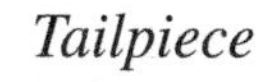

Tailpiece

Wag Tails

AS every dog knows from whence they were taught as a young puppy, the history of the world was passed down in '*The Canine Chronicles*'.

Of course, these were not a written source, such as in two paw history, but one that was passed down from doggy generation to doggy generation by 'Word of Woof'.

The 'Wag Tail Salute' – as it was known among the canine population – was the highest honour that fellow dogs could bestow on a fellow 'pack' member. The 'hero' would be greeted by a full 21-woof salute from the assembled canines; as he (or she) went past this guard of honour, the two lines of dogs would turn their backs to the recipient and protrude their different shaped and sized rears into the air with their tails wagging wildly in the wind to show appreciation. These moments were rarely seen in canine history, which only increased the stature of their value as the ultimate doggy honour.

Word of Woof had it that the first 'Wag Tail' honour was created by the dogs of Ancient Rome. Every dog knew that Romulus and Remus were brought up and educated by superior four pawed wolves (ancestors of the modern dog) before the two pawed twins founded the ancient city.

Patchus Superbus was the first dog to be honoured with the 'Wag Tail' after he single-pawedly saved Rome itself from being invaded by uncivilised hordes of barbarians (or catarians, as they were known then), led by a vicious monster called Genghis Fang.

With the barbarians at the gates of the city, only one bridge separated the invaders from the dogged defenders. As a two paw called Horatio fought off the barbarians, Patchus Superbus bravely bit into the ropes holding the bridge, despite the spears, arrows and catty remarks being flung at him by the enemy from across the Tiber. As the leading barbarian was about to put his foot on the sacred soil of Rome, Patchus Superbus bit through the last strand of rope supporting the bridge and it, and the barbarians, fell into the river where all the latter drowned.

For his daring actions Patchus Superbus was honoured with the first ever salute of a Wag Tail on the Forum by the grateful canis of Rome.

As he was inspecting the wagging rears he was accompanied, respectfully two paws behind him, by Slipperonius, a slave dog from the wild tribes of Northern Britannia. It was his job to make sure the hero of the hour did not let all this adoration go to his head and so he whispered in Patchus Superbus's ear – 'You are a mere mortal DOG and not a GOD.'

More than a thousand years later another dog, called Patchiracticus, who belonging to an Anglo-Saxon tribe on the North East coast, was the first known recipient in the British Isles of the honour.

Led by Eric the Ready, a large scale Viking invasion took place in 809AD, with a fleet of ships which had set off from Scandinavia and sailed across the North Sea to the Northumberland coast.

The loyal Patchiracticus for once had left his owner – who was a trench digger with the Anglo-Saxon army – in order to pursue, in a heat of passion, a cute collie bitch called Emmax who belonged to an itinerant Romany family.

Every night Patchiracticus would howl outside the Romany camp to call to his beloved Emmax, but his advances were only rewarded with buckets of dirty water thrown over him by her fed-up owners. It was while he trotted off to a nearby beach to reflect on his unrequited love that Patchiracticus, purely by chance, was the first to witness the moonlight landing by the marauding Norsemen.

As 'Word of Woof' has it, Eric the Ready was the first to put his two paws down after jumping from the Viking longboat. However, as he did, Patchiracticus, who was already in a foul mood from his spurned romance, ran up to bite the mighty Viking on his ankle.

Eric the Ready howled in pain and took a swipe with his sword at the accursed cur who had the temerity to attack him; fortunately for Patchiracticus, and unfortunately for the invaders, he missed.

'*The Canine Chronicles*' state that after this infamous encounter henceforth the Viking leader was known, among his fellow Norsemen, as Eric the Livid.

Patchiracticus, quickly forgetting his lost love Emmax ('there were plenty more dogfish in the sea', he concluded), then made the famous run back to his master who was with the gathering Anglo-Saxon army encamped inland. In what was the first recorded 'dogathon' he ran, without stop, through a mountain pass exactly 26 miles 385 yards to find his master and warn him of Eric the Livid and his army. Thanks to Patchiracticus's gallantry the large Anglo-Saxon force was able to repel the Viking invasion.

However, the marathon run proved too much for the brave little canine hero, who died in his master's arms from exhaustion.

At his funeral he was honoured with a 'sword of honour' by the two paws as well as, ironically, a Viking funeral, and by the more civilised four paws, with a deserving 'Wag Tail Salute'.

Then, of course, in more recent history, just over 100 years ago, there was another dog that had helped save the nation in its hour of danger.

Unlike the unreliable sources of the two paw versions the more accurate and factual '*The Canine Chronicles*' history tells the tail (tale) of a beloved dog owned by none other than the great Admiral Horatio Nelson himself – another Horatio! So fond was he of his little terrier, that he had found as a stray puppy roaming the quayside of Plymouth, that wherever the admiral went so did the little dog. Much to the embarrassment of Lady Hamilton but that's another tail (tale)!

It was at the Battle of Trafalgar in 1805 when a salty sea dog named One-Eyed Patch – so called because so fond was the admiral of his pet that his fellow sailors on board HMS *Victory* made an eye patch for the four paw to be put over his right eye, in emulation of his esteemed master. The little dog was indeed proud of his distinctive look as it set him aside from all the other sea dogs in His Majesty's Royal Navy – although this was not necessary, as he was already

One-Eyed Patch dressed up as his hero and owner Admiral Horatio Nelson.

recognisable, having only three legs. He had lost a leg from a shard of cannonball when just a young pup at the Battle of Santa Cruz in Tenerife in 1797 against the Spanish and French forces, according to the chronicles. It coincided with his master losing an arm after being shot by musket fire.

Legend has it that two years later, when he was in Naples after the famous British naval victory at the Battle of Aboukir Bay, the dog was chased back to his ship in the harbour by an irate butcher after One-Eyed Patch had 'press ganged' a string of sausages from his shop. The ever-hungry terrier began to eat them on the quayside next to the ship in dock when the shopkeeper waved his fists in rage and complained in a stream of nefarious Neapolitan to the admiral that he must pay for the stolen sausages. Admiral Nelson, looking down from the bridge, put his telescope to his eye and on to the insatiable culprit, before famously declaring: 'I see no sausages.'

The incident put Anglo-Neapolitan relations back for years.

According to two paw history, the Battle of Trafalgar in October 1805 off the Spanish mainland between the ships of the Royal Navy and the combined fleets of the French and Spanish would determine who would be 'top sea dog' to rule the waves. If the British lost there would be nothing to stop Napoleon and his armies from having the maritime capability of cutting off British trade and starving the nation into submission, or even invading England itself. The fate of Europe itself lay at its outcome.

What, of course, the two paws had, once again, failed to record, was the vital role played by One-Eyed Patch in the decisive battle.

In fact, the little terrier had already left his paw print on history. On the eve of Trafalgar, the great admiral was outlining his battle tactics and plan of attack to his captains and senior officers aboard HMS *Victory* – showing them his charts, which were spread across the cabin table. His inquisitive dog, anxious to be in on the action – and who, a few moments before, had his paws in the barrel of the ship's victuals – hopped onto the table. Unfortunately for One-Eyed Patch, this time he over-stepped the mark and left a paw print fresh from the pork barrel on his master's charts. Admiral Nelson was not pleased and threatened to 'clap the offender in irons if he invaded the pork barrel again.' One-Eyed Patch was despatched from the cabin forthwith with a flea in his ear – which was not an unusual condition for the sea dog, along with weevils in his biscuits.

Even today, with the famous charts kept for national posterity in the archives of Admiralty House in London, One-Eyed Patch's paw print can clearly be seen spoiling Nelson's famous battle plan. Forever in '*The Canine Chronicles*' it was known as the 'One-Eyed Patch Touch'.

So cross was his master Admiral Nelson that, at the last minute, in his famous flag signal to his sailors to spur them on before the battle, he changed the words 'England expects every sea dog to do his duty' to a less all embracing 'England expects every man to do his duty.' It was a typically biased declaration by a two paw historian – according to 'Word of Woof' – downgrading the actual contribution of all the dogs on board His Majesty's naval ships and their vital role in this most important of all sea battles.

However, the next day the terrier's transgression was forgiven. According to '*The Canine Chronicles*' at the height of the battle, with the French ships surrounding the valiant HMS *Victory*, there was a point when the enemy forces looked certain to capture the British flagship itself.

A boarding party from the French warship *Redoubtable* managed to throw grappling irons on to the foredeck and their marines, along with a detachment of poodles, prepared to board. If they could take the British flagship and capture the famous Admiral Nelson himself, all would be lost. With many of the British sailors and sea dogs preoccupied fighting off the attack on two sides, this 'weak spot' had gone unnoticed by human eye – however, not to the one good eye of our canine hero.

As a brave French lieutenant leading the boarding party put his hand onto the ship's rail and was ready to board, One-Eyed Patch leapt onto the wooden rail and sank his teeth into the Froggie's (as they said in those less politically correct days) fingers, which drew a loud curse from their owner – his words did not need the necessary translation; he immediately let go and fell into the water.

A few loud barks from the terrier brought a score of Jack Tars with sword and pistol in hand to his rescue, and soon the Gallic hordes ready to board were repelled.

According to Word of Woof, such was the fury of the French that a musketeer sharpshooter in a crow's nest on the *Redoubtable* was ordered by the French Admiral Villeneuve himself to fire at One-Eyed Patch. Despite his superb shot, not made easy by the rolling seas, he only managed to hit his target in the peg leg but it was enough to send One-Eyed Patch crashing face first on the floor. However, having missed his prime prey the disgruntled marksman reloaded for a second shot and had his reward when he hit the nearby

British Seadog One-Eyed Patch
ready to repel all boarders from the dock of
HMS Victory at the Battle of Trafalgar.

Nelson himself – who had come onto the deck at the unfortunate moment in search of his beloved dog – and the admirable admiral was shot in the shoulder and spine.

As the flags were being hoisted by the British to announce victory and cheers went up from their gallant sailors and sea dogs from across the battle lines, the severely injured admiral was taken below deck to the ship's surgeon.

Dying from his fatal wounds he was surrounded by his officers and men, included his loyal lieutenant, Captain Hardy. Two paw historians claimed the great man's final words before he died were 'Kiss me Hardy'. Not true! According to the far more accurate and reliable Word of Woof, his actual words were 'Lick me Patch' and after his loyal furry friend gave a big 'wet un' across his master's face, Admiral Nelson rolled his eyes and England's greatest fighting hero weighed anchor and set sail for 'the Great Cabin in the Sky'.

One-Eyed Patch was distraught at the loss of his beloved master – in fact, he did not eat for nearly four hours – an unprecedented length of time to go without his 'vitals' as he called it.

Following the Battle of Trafalgar and after surviving the 'Great Storm', HMS *Victory* sheltered in Gibraltar for repairs. The flagship then sailed for England, with the body of Admiral Nelson preserved in a brandy barrel. Such was One-Eyed Patch's dedication to his master that he refused to leave his side on the long journey. Unfortunately the dog's only consolation was dipping into the brandy cask when he was thirsty, and soon the little terrier was rolling like a drunken sailor all over the deck in a storm ridden Bay of Biscay.

News of the heroic victory, the death of the great Admiral

and the brave exploits of the loyal One-Eyed Patch had already spread to England before HMS *Victory* had returned home.

Indeed, again because of the inaccuracies of the unreliable two paw version, it was not Greenwich where HMS *Victory* berthed on her return but to Britain's premier naval port of Plymouth.

It was here, when all the dogs of Plymouth's Barbican heard of Patch's home coming arrival, that they rushed to muster at the quayside to greet their canine hero.

The three-legged One-Eyed Patch was on deck and as he disembarked (a sea dog naval term) and hopped down the gangplank, a 29-bark salute was 'fired' from the quayside – the first and only known such numbered bark salute in canine history.

There then followed the esteemed 'Wag Tail Salute' by the doggy population of that fine maritime city. It was rumoured it brought a tear to the eye of One-Eye Patch but this could not be confirmed by canine chroniclers as nobody could see it because of his 'imitation' eye patch.

Despite this moment of glory for Britain's finest sea dog, the zenith of his naval career, he was distraught at the death of his beloved master and life was never again the same for our dogged hero.

Now well into middle age, with his tummy at full sail, his equally growing renown only brought green-eyed (and brown and blue-eyed) envy from lesser dogs with masters in the Admiralty. Shamefully – and some would say a most catty thing to stoop to – they put their two penn'eth worth (actually it was a farthing in those days) in with their masters and One-Eyed Patch never went to sea again, as they nefariously claimed he was 'unfit for duty'.

However, as a mark of respect and now a national hero – he even had numerous public houses named after him and his picture swung from many a pub sign – One-Eyed Patch was given an 'honourable discharge' from His Majesty's Royal Navy.

The terrier was also given a share of the bounty that was the entitlement of sailors and sea dogs that had fought at Trafalgar – in One-Eyed Patch's case a barrel of not so rancid pork and a chest of ship's tack biscuits (without the weevils).

He was also given a small pension of a grog of rum a day and four sausages a week. Unfortunately for One-Eyed Patch his liking for alcohol had been distilled on that fateful sea voyage on the way back home from Trafalgar when escorting his master's pickled remains. From then on Patch began his liking for a tipple and remained himself 'pickled' for the rest of his life.

He ended his days roaming the streets of Devonport cadging slops from compassionate sailors, hopping on his peg-leg from pub to pub; without a crew to take care of him he slept where he could, hankering for his next drop of brandy. Many a time Patch would be found literally legless – or double legless in his case.

Unfortunately he was diagnosed by a sawbone (sea dog language for a ship's doctor) as suffering from what one would call nowadays 'post-traumatic stress'. After the many cruel sights he had witnessed as a fighting sea dog, One-Eyed Patch got into many harbourside fights with fellow sea and civilian dogs, fuelled by his over indulgence of the 'grog'.

He earned a reputation as being a successful street brawler, aided by his tenacious terrier spirit and other spirits.

In fact, according to 'Word of Woof' it was One-Eyed Patch, when pinning the paws of his opponent behind them, who termed the wrestling phase 'a half-Patch' – something he was very proud of, which two paws later 'stole' and claimed it to be 'a half-Nelson'.

Sadly, in one drunken stupor too many, one Saturday night One-Eyed Patch fell off the quay of the Barbican. Unfortunately for him, like many a Jack Tar in his Majesty's Royal Navy, Patch was unable to swim and he was pulled down into the waters of Plymouth Sound by the weight of his peg-leg and a full stomach due to eating his week's ration of sausages in one go. It was a tragic ending as recorded in '*The Canine Chronicles*' but it could not distract from his legendary status as Britain's finest sea dog, which remains to this day.